The Translator

Acclaim for Leila Aboulela's *The Translator*

'A story of love and faith all the more moving for the restraint with which it is written.'

J. M. Coetzee, Booker Prize Winner 1999

'. . . a lyrical journey about exile, loss and love . . . poetry in motion.'

The Sunday Times

'Aboulela is a wonderfully poetic writer: it's a pleasure to read a novel so full of feeling and yet so serene.'

The Guardian

'. . . she pulls you into her world as she refracts British life, its smells and sounds, its advertisements and turns of phrase . . .'

The Independent

'. . . [an] extraordinary first novel . . .'

The Herald

'. . . the first halal novel written in English!'

The Muslim News

'*The Translator* is an enveloping story of the tentative possibilities between a man and a woman, and between faiths; two people, and perhaps peoples, between nations. It is an apt, resonant caution filled with love and poignant understanding of the world. It is exactly what fiction ought to be.'

Todd McEwen

Acclaim for Leila Aboulela's *Coloured Lights*

One of the stories in the collection, 'The Museum' won the inaugural 'African Booker', the Caine Prize for African Writing. It was described by Ben Okri as 'moving, gentle, ironic, quietly angry and beautifully written.'

The Translator

Leila Aboulela

Introduction by Anne Donovan

First published in 1999 reprinted in 2001, 2002, 2005, 2008, 2013
New edition published in 2008 by Polygon an imprint of Birlinn Ltd
West Newington House
10 Newington Road
Edinburgh
www.polygonbooks.co.uk

A CIP Record for this book is
available from the British Library

ISBN 13: 978 1 84697 080 1

Typeset by Hewer Text (UK) Ltd, Edinburgh.

Printed and bound in Great Britain by Clays Ltd, St Ives PLC

INTRODUCTION

T he Translator is a most lyrical and graceful novel. It depicts the emotional journey of a young widow, Sammar, portray-ing her internal life with deep compassion and sensitivity. Leila Aboulela's work is characterised by the extreme beauty of her prose and she describes the domestic and natural world in a way that is at once intensely poetic and utterly readable. We are taken into Sammar's mind and heart, see things from her perspective, and follow her progress from the physical and emotional darkness of her life in Aberdeen to the colour and warmth of Khartoum. At the start of the novel Sammar is lonely and unhappy. Deva-stated by the sudden death of her husband four years previously, separated from her young son and family in Khartoum, she works as a translator at the university in Aberdeen. In typically clear and refined prose the author describes Sammar's grief at her husband's death:

> . . . her invisible mark . . . Four years ago this mark had crystallised. Grief had formed, taken shape, a diamond shape, its four angles stapled on to her forehead, each shoulder, the top of her stomach. She knew it was translucent, she knew that it held a mercurial liquid which flowed up and down

slowly when she moved. The diamond shape of grief made sense to her: her forehead – that was where it hurt when she cried, that space behind her eyes; her shoulders – because they curled to carry her heart. And the angle at the top of her stomach – that was where the pain was.

Sammar feels isolated in Aberdeen: the grey streets and bleak weather are alien to her and she does not understand the habits and customs of the people around her. Above all she is mystified by a culture which does not recognise the presence of God. The only comfort she finds is in conversations with Rae Isles, the professor in her department. He is an expert on the Middle East, but his interest in Islam is academic. He takes an objective stance on something which, to Sammar, one cannot be objective about. She finds it hard to understand how, knowing so much about Islam, he cannot take the final step and profess his faith.

When she visits Rae's house with Yasmin, the departmental secretary, she realises that 'she had not been in a real home for a long time'.

Sammar has been traumatised by the death of her beloved husband, Tarig; frozen in grief, she has nothing in her room.

She lived in a room with nothing on the wall, nothing personal, no photographs, no books; just like a hospital room.

In Rae's company Sammar opens to the possibility of a renewal of her life. Their relationship progresses gradually and is handled with extreme delicacy. Sammar feels that Rae is different from the other people she meets in Scotland, he feels familiar to her. Yasmin puts this down to his being an 'orientalist', a term Sammar dislikes – 'Orientalists were the people who distorted the image of the Arabs and Islam' – though she comforts herself with the thought that 'maybe modern orientalists were different'.

Sammar feels close to Rae because of his feeling for and interest in Islam. Rae tells her that this interest sprang initially from his uncle, who converted to Islam after living in the Middle East, but Yasmin warns Sammar against harbouring any dreams that Rae will also convert. According to her it would be 'professional suicide'. Rae would not be taken seriously if he were actually a Muslim. One of the ironies of western society's attitude to religion is that you can only be an expert if you maintain a distance from it. Sammar's religion and belief in Allah are central to her life and one of the book's great strengths is the way Aboulela depicts the internal life of a devoutly religious person.

Sammar finds it strange to live in a society where people do not pray openly. For her prayer is natural and essential; during the bleakness of the time after Tarig's death it was what kept her going.

> Days in which the only thing she could rouse herself to do was pray the five prayers. They were the only challenge, the last touch with normality, without them she would have fallen, lost awareness of the shift of day into night.

Now she lives in a society where people do and say all kinds of private things in public but prayer must be kept hidden.

> On days when Diane was not in, Sammar prayed in the room, locking the door from inside . . . It had seemed strange for her when she first came to live here, all that privacy that surrounded praying. She was used to seeing people pray on pavements and on grass. She was used to praying in the middle of parties, in places where others chatted, slept or read.

Sammar also finds it difficult to come to terms with the way in which western people seem to live as though they were fully agents of their own destiny; for her there is a divine plan. When she discusses this with Rae he says:

> . . . in this secular society, the speculation is that God is out playing golf . . . that God has put up this elaborate solar system and left it to run itself. It does not need Him to maintain it or sustain it in anyway. Mankind is self-sufficient.

For those around her this self-sufficiency equates to freedom, but for Sammar, faith is liberation.

> My fate is etched out by Allah Almighty, if and who I will marry, what I eat, the work I find, my health, the day I will die are as He alone wants them to be. To think otherwise was to slip down, to feel the world narrowing, dreary and tight.

It is not simply an intellectual acquiescence which Sammar feels; her belief that her life is in the hands of a divine power makes her emotionally and physically whole.

During the Christmas holidays, Sammar and Rae become closer through a series of phone calls. The rented apartment where Sammar lives is quieter than usual and she is able to sit in the hallway, talking on the pay phone. Not being face to face liberates them and they speak openly, Rae talking about his experiences in the Middle East and Sammar telling him of her life in Khartoum. Gradually their intimacy increases; he tells her of a stillborn child from a previous relationship, while Sammar talks of her son. The development of their relationship causes an awakening in Sammar. She realises the way she has allowed things to slide since the death of her husband.

> She opened cupboards and drawers to find tired elastic, worn-out nylon and scruffy shoes with eroded heels. She

held these things in her hand as if seeing them for the first time. Frayed wools, discoloured cottons and even her scarves, the silks for her hair which she had always chosen with care were now dull and threadbare. Since Tarig died she had not bought anything new. She had not noticed time moving past, the years eroding the clothes Tarig had seen her in, wools he had touched, colours he had given his opinion on.

She buys a new coat, clears her room and puts up fresh curtains. Psychologically she is prepared for a new beginning but when she goes back to work after the holidays she discovers that Rae is in hospital, suffering from bronchitis.

Sammar's visit to Rae is an important turning point. Up till now the tentative steps they have taken towards each other have been private; shielded by the telephone, they have not even looked at each others' faces. Not only will being in the hospital bring up memories of Tarig's death, it will cause a big shift in the intimacy between Rae and Sammar. She considers turning back.

'You can go to him another day,' she told herself, 'when he is more recovered.' Maybe Yasmin could come with you or . . . the other students . . . then it would look more respectable, people from work coming to see him.

However Rae makes it plain by his welcome how happy he is to see her and gives her a gift of a bottle of perfume. And during the visit Rae makes explicit to Sammar his feelings about the Qur'an.

'I view the Qur'an as a sacred text, as the word of God. It would be impossible in the kind of work I'm doing, in the issues I'm addressing for me to do otherwise but accept Muslims' own vision of the Qur'an, what they say about it.

To Fareed, though, this is tantamount to accepting Islam, and so he can't understand it when I say I am not a Muslim.' Sammar couldn't understand it either.

By now Sammar's feelings for Rae are strong enough that she wants him to convert to Islam in order to marry her, but she simply says, 'It would be good for you, it will make you stronger.'

Through Rae's recommendation, Sammar is to travel to Cairo as a translator for a few weeks; this will allow her to go home to Khartoum for a visit. Just before she is due to leave, Sammar asks Rae to convert to Islam so they can be married. When Rae says he cannot go through the motions of conversion for the sake of marrying Sammar she is angry. She says he should not have allowed things to go so far if his intentions were not clear. Feeling hurt and betrayed, she leaves.

The second part of the book deals with Sammar's return to Khartoum where she lives in her aunt's house, renews her relationship with her family and finds herself again as a mother to her son, Amir. Her homecoming enables her to come to terms properly with the enormity of what has happened to her.

When she cried her aunt and Hanan started to cry . . . Only after they had cried together did the awkwardness of their meeting begin to break, the years she was away. Only then was it reaffirmed she was who she was, Amir's mother, Tarig's widow coming home.

The person Sammar had been in Aberdeen, the translator living in her single room, with no real friends or life of her own, has gone. In Khartoum she is surrounded by family and living in a society where Allah is central to life. Although her relationship with her aunt is problematic and she misses Rae desperately, Sammar decides she is not going back. Her brother is amazed that she does not want to return to Scotland and take Amir with her. When she says she intends to resign from her post at the university he says:

> You're so fortunate. A good job, a civilised place. None of these power cuts and strikes and what not . . . what's the matter with you?

It is impossible for Sammar to explain to her brother why she cannot bear to go back to Aberdeen, but the author reveals it to us, using Sammar's perception of the natural world to throw light on her internal state. The rain and cold of Aberdeen are delineated with precision:

> . . . a grey October sky. Scottish grey with mist from the North Sea.
> A still day with a downcast sky, no sun.

Sammar is fearful of the rain and fog and snow; it keeps her indoors, trapped in her little room. The grey of Scotland is contrasted with the colour of Khartoum, where, in spite of her internal turmoil and the privations mentioned by her brother, Sammar is free to enjoy the outside space.

> She could have all the colours she had missed in Aberdeen; yellow and brown, and everything else vivid. Flat land and a peaceful emptiness; space, no grey, no wind, no lines of granite. The sun had rimmed the houses down the road and left behind layers of pink and orange. In the east there was the confident blue of night, a flimsy moon, one two, three stars . . . On the other side of the road, the night-watchman of the co-operative was serving his friends tea. They sat on the pavement on a large palm-fibre mat; prayer beads and laughter. Coals glowed, a kettle of water boiled and let

off steam in the twilight. Her homesickness was cured, her eyes cooled by what she saw, the colours and how the sky was so much bigger than the world below, transparent.

The section in Khartoum forms a beautiful parallel with the first section and her return to her home enables the completion of the healing process begun by her relationship with Rae. I do not wish to spoil the reader's enjoyment by giving away the ending of the book but it is marked by the sensitive understanding of human nature and delicacy of touch which characterises all Leila Aboulela's work. *The Translator* is an utter joy to read; a novel to savour and treasure.

Anne Donovan
February 2008

PART ONE

But I say what comes to me
From my inner thoughts
Denying my eyes.

Abu Nuwas (757–814)

I

*

S e dreamt that it rained and she could not go out to meet him as planned. She could not walk through the hostile water, risk blurring the ink on the pages he had asked her to translate. And the anxiety that she was keeping him waiting pervaded the dream, gave it an urgency that was astringent to grief. She was afraid of rain, afraid of the fog and the snow which came to this country, afraid of the wind even. At such times she would stay indoors and wait, watching from her window people doing what she couldn't do: children walking to school through the swirling leaves, the elderly smashing ice on the pavement with their walking sticks. They were superhuman, giants who would not let the elements stand in their way. Last year when the city had been dark with fog, she hid indoors for four days, eating her way through the last packet of pasta in the cupboard, drinking tea without milk. On the fifth day when the fog lifted she went out famished, rummaging the shops for food, dizzy with the effort.

But Sammar's dream was wrong. It wasn't raining when she woke that morning, a grey October sky, Scottish grey with mist from the North Sea. And she did go out to meet Rae Isles as planned, clutching her blue folder with the translation of *Al-Nidaa*'s manifesto.

The door to the Winter Gardens (an extended greenhouse in Duthie Park) was covered with signs. *Sorry, no prams or pushchairs allowed, sorry, no dogs allowed, opening hours 9.30 till dusk.* In this country everything was labelled, everything had a name. She had got used to the explicitness, all the signs and polite rules. It was 9.30 now and when they went inside there was only a gardener pushing a wheel-barrow along the wet cracked slabs that separated the plants. Tropical plants cramped in the damp warmth and orange fish in running water. Whistling birds flying indoors, the grey sky irrelevant above the glass ceiling.

Benches. White curved metal, each and every one bore a placard, In Loving Memory of this person or that. As if people must die so that others can sit in the Winter Gardens. People must die . . . Her invisible mark shifted, breathed its existence. It was hidden from Rae, like her hair and the skin on her arms, it could only be imagined. Four years ago this mark had crystal-lised. Grief had formed, taken shape, a diamond shape, its four angles stapled on to her forehead, each shoulder, the top of her stomach. She knew it was translucent, she knew that it held a mercurial liquid which flowed up and down slowly when she moved. The diamond shape of grief made sense to her: her forehead – that was where it hurt when she cried, that space behind her eyes; her shoulders – because they curled to carry her heart. And the angle at the top of her stomach – that was where the pain was.

So that she was somewhat prepared, now that the liquid in the diamond moved carefully like oil and was not surprised when Rae asked her about Tarig. 'My aunt's son,' she replied, 'but it was not until I was seven that I met him. I was born here as you know and my parents and I did not go back home until I was seven.'

They were sitting on a bench in a room full of cacti. The cacti were like rows of aliens in shades of green, of different heights, standing still, listening. They were surrounded by sand for the room was meant to give the impression of a desert. The light was different too, airier, more yellow.

'Not until I was seven.' These were her words, the word 'until' as if she still could not reconcile herself to those first seven years of life without him. In better times she used to reinvent the beginnings of her life. Make believe that she was born at home in Sudan, Africa's largest land, in the Sisters' Maternity Hospital, delivered by a nun dressed in white. She liked to imagine that Tarig was waiting for her outside the delivery room, holding his mother's hand, impatient for her, a little fidgety. Perhaps she would have been given a different name had she been born in Khartoum, a more common one. A name suggested by her aunt, for she was a woman who had an opinion on all things. Sammar was the only Sammar at school and at college. When people talked about her they never needed to use her last name. 'Do you pronounce it like the season, summer?' Rae asked the first time she had met him. 'Yes, but it does not have the same meaning.' And because he wanted to know more she said, 'It means conversations with friends, late at night. It's what the desert nomads liked to do, talk leisurely by the light of the moon, when it was no longer so hot and the day's work was over.'

Rae knew the Sahara, knew that most Arabic names had familiar meanings. He was a Middle-East historian and a lecturer in Third World Politics. He had recently written a book called *The Illusion of an Islamic Threat*. When he appeared on TV or was quoted in a newspaper he was referred to as an Islamic expert, a label he disliked because, he told Sammar, there could be no such monolith. Sammar was the translator in Rae's department. She worked on several projects at the same time, historical texts, newspaper articles in Arab newspapers, and now a political manifesto Rae had given her. *Al-Nidaa* were an extremist group in the south of Egypt. The document was handwritten, badly photocopied and full of spelling mistakes. It was stained with tea and what she guessed to be beans mashed with oil. Last night she had stayed up late transforming the Arabic rhetoric into English, imagining she could smell beans cooked in the way she had known long ago, with cumin and olive oil, all the time trying not to think too much about the meeting next day, not to make a big thing out of it.

Among the cacti, Rae had queried 'Tariq?', stressing the q. She answered, 'Yes, it's written with a *qaf* but we pronounce the *qaf* as a g back home.' He nodded, he knew the letters of the Arabic alphabet, he had lived in her part of the world. Rae looked like he could easily pass for a Turk or a Persian. He was dark enough. He had told her once that in Morocco he could walk as if disguised, none suspected he was Scottish as long as he did not speak and let his pronunciation give him away. Here with others, he looked to her to be out of place, not only because of his looks but his manners. The same manners which made her able to talk to him, made the world vivid for the first time in years. The last time she had met him she had gone home ill: eyelids heavy as coins, hammers beating her head, the smallest ray of light agony to her eyes. When she stumbled into unconsciousness and woke up feeling radiant, light, she thought she must have had something like an epileptic fit.

'Tarig's mother, my aunt, is called Mahasen,' she went on, wondering which part of the narrative to soften, to omit. How much of the truth could he take, without a look of surprise crossing his eyes? She had never said anything that surprised him before. And she wanted it always to be like that. In this country, when she spoke to people, they seemed wary, on their guard as if any minute she would say something out of place, embarrassing. He was not like that. He seemed to understand, not in a modern, deliberately non-judgemental way but as if he was about to say, 'This has happened to me too.'

When she boiled chicken, froth rose to the surface of the water and she removed it with a spoon. It was granulated dirt the colour of peanuts, scum from the chicken that was better not eaten. Inside Sammar there was froth like that, froth that could rise if she started to speak. Then he would see it and maybe go away, when what she wanted was for him to remove it so that she could be clear. It would be easy for him to make her clear, she thought, as easy as untying a ribbon.

Tell him, she told herself, tell him of Mahasen and Tarig and Hanan. Mother, son, daughter. Tell him how you shrugged off your own family and attached yourself to them, the three of them. Made a gift of yourself, a child to be moulded. Their house, where you imagined you would one day live, the empty square in front of it. When it rained, everything stood still and the square took the colour of the moon. Tarig's bike, Tarig's room, Tarig singing with imaginary microphones, imaginary guitars, imaginary drums. An obedient niece, letting Mahasen decide how you should dress, how you should fix your hair. You were happy with that, content, waiting for the day you would take her only son away from her. 'Take care of Tarig,' she whispered in your ear when you said goodbye. And you brought him back to her shrouded in the belly of an airplane.

'My aunt is a strong woman,' Sammar said, 'a leader really. She is looking after my son now. I haven't seen them for four years.' She had given the child to Mahasen and it had not meant anything, nothing, as if he had not been once a piece of her, with her wherever she walked. She was unable to mother the child. The part of her that did the mothering had disappeared. Froth, ugly froth. She had said to her son, 'I wish it was you instead. I hate you. I hate you.' In that same death-carrying airplane he had wanted to play, toddle up and down the aisles, all smiles, his father's ease with strangers. He had wanted food, he was greedy for food. On her lap with the tray precarious before them, he had grabbed rolls of bread, smeared butter, poured the juice on her clothes. Full of life, they said of him, full of life. She pinched him hard when no one was looking. He kicked her back. In the bathroom she cleaned him while he wriggled, his hands reaching for the ashtray, the button that called the hostess. Stop it, stop it. The child would not let her be, would not let her sink like she wanted to sink, bend double with pain. He demanded her totally.

'Tarig was a student here,' she said. 'We came here after we got married. He was a medical student and we lived near Foresterhill. On the day the car accident happened and he was taken to hospital, some of the doctors on duty there knew him. They were very good to me. They called the Ethnic Minority . . .,' she stopped, 'Worker or Coordinator,' she wasn't sure what the woman's title was. Rae shrugged, it didn't matter. He wiped his face with the palm of his hand, down to his chin and up to press his fingers against his temples.

The coordinator was an energetic woman with curly hair. In the stark, white moments of disbelief, she took the roaming, exploring child, saddled him on her hips and bought him Maltesers from the snack machine. 'This one is for you, Mama,' he said when he came back, teeth stained with melted brown. He lifted the sweet to her closed lips, made coaxing noises like the ones she made when she fed him. 'No, not now, it is for you, all for you.' She could see the woman on the telephone, gesticulating with her hands. The child whined in anger, stamped his foot, pushed the chocolate against her lips. Against her will she bit into its hushed sweetness, honeycomb and tears. 'That woman was the one who called the mosque and someone from there came to do . . . to do the washing.'

A whole week passed before she got him under African soil. It had taken that long to arrange everything through the embassy in London: the quarantine, the flight. People helped her, took over. Strangers, women whom she kept calling by the wrong names, filled the flat, cooked for her and each other, watched the ever-wandering child so she could cry. They prayed, recited the Qur'an, spent the night on the couch and on the floor. They did not leave her alone, abandoned. She went between them dazed, thanking them, humbled by the awareness that they were stronger than her, more giving than her, though she thought of herself as more educated, better dressed. She covered her hair with Italian silk, her arms with tropical colours. She wanted to look as elegant as Benazir Bhutto, as mesmerising as the Afghan princess she had once seen on TV wearing hijab, the daughter of an exiled leader of the mujahideen. Now the presence of these women kept her sane, held her up. She went between them thanking them, humbled by the awareness that they were not doing this for her or for Tarig, but only because they believed it was the right thing to do.

Their children ran about, her son among them, delighted with the company, excited by the gathering of people. Poor orphan, not yet two, he can't understand, the women said as he leapt past them with a toy car in each fist, trilling the names of his new friends. But it seemed to Sammar cruel and shocking that he would not stop or pause and that with the same undiminished zest he wanted to play and eat and be held so that he could sleep.

Tarig's clothes clung wet with hers in the washing machine between the spin and dry cycle.

When they dried she put them with his other things in a black dustbin bag. Packing and giving things away. She filled black bag after black bag, an evacuation. Tearing letters, dropping magazines in the bin, a furious dismantling of the life they had lived, the home they made. Only Allah is eternal, only Allah is eternal. Photographs, books, towels, sheets. Strip and dump into a black bag. Temporary, this life is temporary, fleeting. Why is this lesson so hard to learn? Pens, boots, a torchlight, a comb. The index cards he used for studying. Could you please take these bags to the mosque, someone might need something . . . A pair of shoes, Tarig's coat that was nearly new. The tape recorder, the little rug . . . Strip, give away, pack. We're going home, we're finished here, we're going to Africa's sand, to dissolve in Africa's sand.

How did she bring herself to phone Mahasen? To be the bearer of the worst news? And Mahasen's phone was not working. It had to be the neighbour's and Mahasen running, breathless, a tobe flung over her nightdress, one roller perched at the top of her head like a purple crest. She was always like that at home, with this one purple roller in her hair. She even slept with it so that when she went out a fringe would peep becomingly from under her tobe.

'I love your mother more than you,' she had teased him, hugging her aunt, kissing her cheeks, putting her head on her shoulder. 'Go away, Tarig, we want to talk,' she would say laughing. 'We are going to gossip about you,' Mahasen would say to him, 'in little pieces.' The word for 'gossip' meant cutting, too.

This was the Mahasen who now frowned when mentioning Sammar's name. 'That idiot girl.'

2

'*Euphorbia Herimentiana, Cereus Peruvianus, Hoya Carnosa.*' Rae read out loud the names of the cacti. Names that Sammar could not pronounce. '*Cleistocactus Reae*, planted by Silvana Suarez, Miss World 1979. Really?' He made a face. It made Sammar smile. It was the second time she had seen him outside work and it still felt strange. New and happy like seeing a baby walk for the first time.

The first time had been Saturday when she went to the public library with Yasmin. Yasmin was Rae's secretary. A glass door connected her office with Rae's so that when Sammar went to see him, she could see, while they talked, Yasmin furiously typing, her straight black hair hiding her face. Yasmin's parents were from Pakistan but she was born and had lived all her life in different parts of Britain. She had a habit of making general statements starting with 'we', where 'we' meant the whole of the Third World and its people. So she would say, 'We are not like them', or 'We have close family ties, not like them.' There were two other department secretaries who worked in the same room as Yasmin: cheerful, coffee-scented ladies with greying hair and pleated skirts. When one of them once patted the curves of her stomach and bemoaned the fact that she could not stick long to any diet, Yasmin was quick to say, 'Our children are dying of hunger while the rich count their calories!'

Yasmin's husband, Nazim, worked some of the time on the oilrigs off-shore. When he was away, she tended to meet Sammar at the weekends. Yasmin had a car and Sammar liked driving around, listening to the radio, seeing parts of the city she had not seen before. She wished she could have a car and escape the weather.

That Saturday, they went to the library because Yasmin, now ten weeks pregnant, wanted to look at baby books. There were shelves of books about pregnancy, birth, breastfeeding. The library was warm, full of people, full of books. There were books on Caesarean birth, abortions, infertility and miscarriage. Sammar had miscarried once, a year after her son was born. She remembered the night, fateful and climactic, coming after days of anxiety, days of awareness that this pregnancy was not going right, something was wrong. She remembered Tarig being calm, warm and sure of what to do. She remembered him on his hands and knees mopping the bathroom floor, her womb that had fallen apart.

There was gratitude between them. Gratitude cushioned the quarrels, petty and deep. It levelled the dips in affection. Sometimes this gratitude came to her in trances and in dreams. Dreams with neither settings nor narratives, just the feeling, distilled.

'I can only take six books,' Yasmin was saying. 'If you had a card I could borrow on yours. That's an idea. Let's get you a card.'

'No, some other time.' She did not like doing things impulsively, without warning. She looked at the queues which stretched out from the desk, the librarians running pens over the barcodes on the books. They made her nervous. She tried to sound convincing. 'You'll never read more than six books in a month. Six is enough.'

But Yasmin insisted, giving her a lecture on how a library card was a right. 'You pay tax, don't you?' she said and told her how a Nigerian woman with three children had lived in Aberdeen for seven years before finding out that she was entitled to Child Benefit. 'No one told her,' Yasmin screeched in a whisper.

Twelve books on pregnancy made their way to the counter. Yasmin did all the talking. Sammar felt like a helpless immigrant who didn't know any English. She imagined the English words lifting away from her brain, evaporating, forming a light mist. It was one of the things that Mahasen had said to her the night of their quarrel, almost trembling with anger, fluent with right-eousness. The night when Sammar had asked her permission to marry Ahmad Ali Yasseen. *An educated girl like you, you know English . . . you can support yourself and your son, you don't need marriage. What do you need it for? He started to talk to me about this and I silenced him. I shamed him, the old fool.* 'He's religious,' Sammar had choked the words, 'he feels a duty towards widows . . .' *He can take his religiousness and build a mosque but keep away from us. In the past, widows needed protection, life is different now.* She had wanted to say something in reply but the words stuck in her throat like dough.

'Rae's book,' said Yasmin, just as they were leaving, 'did you see it? I'm sure it's here. Nobody reads these kind of things.' With their twelve books they went back to the History section and searched, finally finding *The Illusion of an Islamic Threat* upstairs, classified under Politics. On the back Sammar read in italics what others said about it, *Brings a new understanding to the turbulent situation in the Middle East . . . – Independent on Sunday. Isles sets out to prove that the threat of an Islamic take-over of the Middle-East is exaggerated . . . his arguments are bold, his insights provocative . . . – The Scotsman.*

They talked about him when they left the library, their voices carrying above the sound of the traffic and the cold wind. Sammar wanted to know about his ex-wives. The first, Yasmin said, was married now and living in Wales. She belonged to the distant past, Yasmin had never met her. The second, the mother of the daughter who was in boarding school in Edinburgh, worked for the World Health Organisation in Geneva. They used to live in Cults, a nice big house. Then he moved to a flat in town.

Yasmin drove erratically, the books slid and parted in the back seat. She parked in a tree-lined street, in a part of town that was unfamiliar to Sammar. 'This is where he lives,' she said. 'I've come here often with Nazim. It's good that you're with me, I can give him these faxes that came for him yesterday after he went home. He's waiting to hear any moment now from the anti-terrorist programme. They're going to take him on as a consultant.'

'We can't do that, it's not right,' said Sammar, 'give them to him on Monday . . .' But Yasmin was already unclasping her seat-belt, switching the heating off, pulling up the hand brake. 'We're together,' she answered, 'it's not as if either of us is on her own.'

'He might not be in anyway,' Sammar went on. Yasmin was out of the car, Sammar still tied in by her seat-belt. It was getting dark, the clouds were plastered purple against the sky, the sun far away.

When Rae opened the door, fur brushed against Sammar's knees. It was a large black cat which made its way indoors with them. Sammar was wary of cats. When she was young stray cats had sneaked indoors and shocked her by jumping out of cupboards or from underneath the stairs. They were savage cats, their ribs visible against matted, dirty fur. Some had a black hole instead of an eye, some had stumpy legs, amputated tails. While she screamed, they ran back and forth in the room, desperately seeking an exit. It seemed to her that they clambered the walls, clawed the paint, cried furiously like she was crying, to get out of the trap they had voluntarily entered and back to the outdoor life they knew.

Tarig had a story about stray cats, the ones that lived around the hospital. 'Their favourite meal,' he said, 'comes every time a baby is born. They wait around the dustbins, one juicy placenta drops in, and you should see how they fight for it!' He liked to tease her with gory hospital stories. Laugh at the expression on her face.

Rae's cat was slow and wellfed. She walked, glossy and serene, around the room while he greeted Yasmin and Sammar and showed them in. 'What happened to your hair!' was the first thing Yasmin said. His hair was cut so short that it stood up from his head like spikes. He laughed and patted his head, saying, 'I guess the barber was over-zealous this time.' He looked different from how he was at work. He was not wearing a tie and had not shaved. It seemed to Sammar that the flat was not very large. The room they sat in was attached to the kitchen. Large bay windows overlooked the road and on the other side of the room, over the kitchen sink, was another window with yellow blinds. There were books lined under the window and the weekend supplement spread out on the floor.

The cat climbed up and sat on Sammar's knees. She did not know what to do, she had not looked at a cat closely like this before, not seen the yellow slits of its iris, the shine on its perfect black coat. She stroked it awkwardly and listened to Yasmin and Rae talking about the faxes, the weather outside, the headlines on the newspaper that Rae now picked up from the floor and folded away. 'I loathe all this fuss about the Royals,' Yasmin was saying. 'Loathe' was another of the words that Yasmin often used. 'I loathe this shitty British weather.'

Rae went to make tea. The cat left Sammar's lap and she began to look around at the rugs on the wall, the copper plant pots on the floor. There was a photograph of Rae's daughter on top of a shelf of books. She looked like she was around ten or eleven and was riding a horse. She wore boots and a cap with straps along her chin. Sammar imagined the child's mother with that same long brown hair, courageous too, working for the WHO, an important job, doing good, helping people.

She thought as she drank her tea that she was in a real home. She had not been in a real home for a long time. She lived in a room with nothing on the wall, nothing personal, no photographs, no books; just like a hospital room. She had given everything away, that week before taking Tarig home. She had stripped everything and given it away, never imagining she would come back, never imagining the quarrel with Mahasen. And when she did come back she had neither the heart nor the means to buy things. Pay the rent for the room and that was all. One plate, one spoon, a tin opener, two saucepans, a kettle, a mug. She didn't care, didn't mind. Four years ill in a hospital she had made for herself. Ill, diseased with passivity, time in which she sat doing nothing. The whirlpool of grief sucking time. Hours flitting away like minutes. Days in which the only thing she could rouse herself to do was pray the five prayers. They were the only challenge, the last touch with normality, without them she would have fallen, lost awareness of the shift of day into night.

She tasted the tea Rae had made for her and listened to the only two people she really knew in this city. Yasmin, her face a little pinched in the early weeks of pregnancy, dark shadows under sleepy eyes. But that was natural, she would be big and healthy in a few months' time, round in maternity clothes. And Rae – it was strange to see people she only knew from work in their own homes. He didn't shave at weekends.

One of the magazines that lay open on the floor had pictures of different world maps. It was an article on traditional maps and how they tended to show continents incorrectly in proportion to one another: Europe appeared larger than South America, North America larger than Africa, Greenland larger than China, when the opposite was true. In the latest, equal-area map, Africa was a massive elongated yellow, Britain a rosy insignificance. Somewhere in this vast yellow, near the blue that marked the flow of the Nile, was the life she had been exiled from.

She knelt and sat on her heels to look more closely. The familiar names of towns, in black type against the yellow, moved her. Kassala, Darfur, Sennar. Kadugli, Karima, Wau. Inside her was their sheer dust and meagreness. Sunshine and poverty. Voices of those who endured because they asked so little of life. On the next page of the magazine there was an advertisement for educational materials. Schoolgirls in Somalia, smiling, arm in arm. Short-sleeved white shirts under a navy pinafore, white belts around their waists. She had dressed like that, been a face like that once. Hair carefully brushed, white socks and the white belt. She remembered walking with friends, her fingers hooked in their belts. Tugging. 'Hurry, the canteen will run out of Bezianous.' The bottles had little bumps all around, pretty curved bumps. The Bezianous was pink and sweet, never cold enough. Smooth the sand under your foot, pat it flat, very flat. Hold the empty bottle, don't cheat and bend your knees, let it drop. If it stands, then what? Your wish will come true, or 'he' loves you too.

When she looked up, Rae was watching her, a look in his eyes like kindness. Encouraged she said, 'I used to wear a uniform like that in secondary school.'

'They made us wear shorts,' he said, 'even in winter. It was awful, walking to school in the cold. I was glad when I got expelled.'

'You got expelled from school?' asked Yasmin. 'What terrible thing did you get up to?'

'I wrote an essay,' he was laughing so that Sammar did not know whether he was joking or not. 'I wrote an essay entitled *Islam is better than Christianity*.'

Yasmin started to laugh. 'Liar, I don't believe you, you're making this up.'

'No, it's true. This was in the fifties. They probably wanted to expel me anyway and this was the last straw.'

'Why did you write something like that?'

'I had an uncle who went to Egypt with the army in the Second World War. When he got there, he became interested in Sufism, converted to Islam, and left the army. You can imagine, he was considered a traitor, a defector. My grandmother told people that he was missing in action. She kept saying it until she believed it and everyone else in the family came to believe it too. Uncle David wrote to her, and to my mother too, explaining why he had done what he did.'

Sammar closed the magazine. Rae sat back in his chair. He coughed and blew his nose in a large blue handkerchief. He looked as if this was a story he told often and liked to tell again. 'I read this letter. It was, I think, the first time I came across the word "Islam" and understood what it meant. Of course I was aware that my uncle had done something scandalous and I was curious. Also I had this essay that I had to write for school. I wish that I still had David's letter now, or even the essay. Because,' and he paused, 'I plagiarised whole paragraphs. The title though was mine. David never of course wrote that Islam was "better" than Christianity. He didn't use that word. Instead he said things like it was a step on, in the way that Christianity followed Judaism. He said that the Prophet Muhammad was the last in a line of prophets that stretched from Adam, to Abraham through Moses and Jesus. They were all Muslims, Jesus was a Muslim, in a sense that he had surrendered to God. This did not go down very well in the letter nor in the essay.'

Rae was laughing again.

'And so what happened to your uncle?' Sammar asked. 'Did he ever come back?'

'He couldn't come back, even if he had wanted to. He would have been arrested. Defection, treason, these are serious charges. He kept writing for some years to my mother. He changed his name, married an Egyptian woman and had children. I had Egyptian cousins, relatives in Africa. I was very excited by that. I thought it was very romantic. But my mother never answered his letters, or maybe sent him nasty letters, in return, so he stopped writing. I went looking for him for five years, between 1976 and '81 when I was in Cairo teaching at the AUC, but I couldn't find him. I wouldn't mind going over to look for him again.'

They were quiet when he finished speaking. Sammar felt that she and Yasmin had been in his flat for a long time. The afternoon in the library seemed distant, another day. The last drops of tea in her mug looked like honey. Then Yasmin started to talk of people's intolerance and Sammar got up to wash the mugs in the kitchen. 'It will only take a minute,' she said to Rae when he told her to leave them, not to bother. But she took her time and looked around. A bottle of Safeway Olive Oil stood on the kitchen counter, an open packet of soluble aspirins, more photographs of the daughter, younger and smiling, were stuck to the door of the fridge. On the wall, there was a print of the Uleg-Beg Mosque in Samarkand, its exterior designed with the interlacing, intricate patterns of Islamic art. It was built in 1418, the caption read, and was both a masjid and a school that taught not only religious sciences but astronomy, mathematics and philosophy. Sammar rolled the blind up over the kitchen window and she could see in the dark a garden shed, lights in the other buildings, the auras of people's lives. Warm water, lather that smelt of lemon, Rae's voice.

'. . . at times the courts here do show cultural sensitivity,' he was saying, 'and each case sets a precedent for others to follow. In one case a High Court judge awarded a divorced Asian woman damages, in thousands of pounds, against her husband. He had slandered her by suggesting she was not a virgin at the time of her marriage. The grounds for the case were that the insult was very serious in her community.'

'Yes, we prize virginity,' Yasmin said, 'and chastity. It's hard to believe that a British judge and jury could understand that, let alone sympathise.'

'People understand it but in the context of its own place, its own part of the world. Here though, it's a different story. I would think that the consensus is "in Rome do as the Romans do".'

'Typical imperialist thinking.'

'You're right,' he said, 'but these things take time to change. Not in our lifetime, I don't think.'

'In *your* lifetime,' said Yasmin. 'We're young, aren't we Sammar?'

Sammar turned around. Her hands were wet with soap and she held them above the sink. 'You're younger than me,' she said to Yasmin.

'I'm going to be thirty next week,' said Yasmin. 'My birthday and Nazim will be away as usual.'

'He's still off-shore?' asked Rae.

'Off Shetland, freezing away, poor thing. But it is so peaceful without him.'

'You say things you don't mean, Yasmin,' said Sammar. She turned off the taps and wiped the basin with the wash cloth. There were stains around the plug and in between the taps.

'Chekhov wrote,' said Rae, 'that a woman pines when she is deprived of the company of a man and when deprived of the company of a woman, a man becomes stupid.'

'Rubbish,' said Yasmin. 'I never pine.'

Sammar looked around for a towel to wipe her hands. The towel she found hanging on the back of a chair had a picture of a dolphin on it. The cat was nowhere in sight. It had gone outside and it was time for them to leave too. 'We should go, shouldn't we?' she said to Yasmin when she joined them, 'It's getting late.'

'I'm so tired I can't move,' Yasmin said and Sammar had to hold both her hands and pull her up.

'What are you going to be like in a few months' time?' she teased her, and they were laughing when Rae opened the front door and walked with them down the steps.

Outside, Sammar stepped into a hallucination in which the world had swung around. Home had come here. Its dimly lit streets, its sky and the feel of home had come here and balanced just for her. She saw the sky cloudless with too many stars, imagined the night warm, warmer than indoors. She smelled dust and heard the barking of stray dogs among the street's rubble and pot-holes. A bicycle bell tinkled, frogs croaked, the muezzin coughed into the microphone and began the azan for the *Isha* prayer. But this was Scotland and the reality left her dulled, unsure of herself. This had happened before but not for so long, not so deeply. Sometimes the shadows in a dark room would remind her of the power cuts at home or she would mistake the gurgle of the central-heating pipes for a distant azan. But she had never stepped into a vision before, home had never come here before. It took time to take in the perfect neatness of the buildings and the gleaming road. It took time for the heating in Yasmin's car to clear the mist of their breath on the window panes.

They drove through streets bright with lamplight, full of cars. Young people strolled along Union Street as if they did not feel the cold. Saturday night, another world.

'Rae is different,' Sammar said. Her voice made it sound like a question.

'In what way?'

'He's sort of familiar, like people from back home.'

'He's an orientalist. It's an occupational hazard.'

Sammar did not like the word orientalist. Orientalists were bad people who distorted the image of the Arabs and Islam. Something from school history or literature, she could not remember. Maybe modern orientalists were different. Her eyesight was becoming blurred. She felt tired, deflated. The headlights of the cars were too bright, round savage circles crossed by swords.

'Do you think he could one day convert?' Mirages shimmered on the asphalt.

Yasmin snorted.'That would be professional suicide.'

'Why?'

'Because no one will take him seriously after that. What would he be? Another ex-hippy gone off to join some weird cult. Worse than a weird cult, the religion of terrorists and fanatics. That's how it would be seen. He's got enough critics as it is: those who think he is too liberal, those who would even accuse him of being a traitor just by telling the truth about another culture.'

'A traitor to what?'

'To the West. You know, the idea that West is best.'

'But you can never tell about people,' said Sammar. 'Look at this uncle of his . . .'

'Are you hoping he would convert so you could marry him?'

'Don't be silly, I was just wondering.' She breathed in and out as if it was an effort. Her eyes ached, her nose ached. 'I was just wondering because he knows so much about Islam . . .'

'This annoys him.'

'What annoys him?'

'That Muslims expect him to convert just because he knows so much about Islam.'

They had reached Sammar's place by then. She could hardly open her eyes to put the key in the lock, light was a source of suffering. And a headache, pain greater than childbirth. Inside, she wanted to hit her head against something to dislodge what was inside. Sleep, which came so easily in this hospital room, in layers and hours, would not come now. The silence, the absence of pain would not come. *Ya Allah, Ya Arham El-Rahimeen.* When sleep finally came it was desperate unconsciousness. She woke up clear, weightless, full of calm. She thought she must have had something between a migraine and a fit.

3

Others walked in the Winter Gardens now. Mid-morning and families were calling out to each other, strolling among the flowers and green plants. A boy ran past Sammar and Rae, holding a red packet of crisps, the arms of his jacket tied round his waist. Her son would be the same age now as this boy. No longer curved like a baby, no longer learning how to talk. A schoolboy. Mahasen had written to her and said, schools here are not what they used to be, you must come and take him back, it would be better for him. Her aunt's letter arrived when the city was covered in fog (even the postman still made his rounds unperturbed in the dark). A year later and Sammar was still paralysed, unresponsive to her son. Froth, ugly froth.

She could not forget what her aunt had said to her, that night when they quarrelled about Ahmad Ali Yasseen, an old family friend. *Nine months have not yet passed, you want to get married again . . . and to whom? A semi-illiterate with two wives and children your age. I'll never give permission for something like this. From what sort of clay have you been made of? Explain to me. Explain what you think you're going to do . . .* Throughout her childhood, 'Am Ahmad had come to visit from the south. A roll of dust behind his Toyota van, crates of mangoes, straps of sugar cane. He laughed happiness.

Sammar always remembered him as laughing, except the time he cried for Tarig, his stomach shaking underneath his white jellabia the same way it did when he laughed. Doctor. He called Tarig 'doctor' even when Tarig was sixteen and waiting for his exam results.

Tarig, Rae had asked about Tarig. There was Ethiopian blood in his family, in the copper hint to his skin, the shape of his nose. Studying for exams, so many exams to become a doctor. Tarig doodling music on his notes. They came to Aberdeen for more exams. Part One, Part Two. Exams that never ended. Culture-shocked they were alone together for the first time. No Mahasen, no Hanan. No one in this new city but them. They had dreamed of this, talked of this. Yet like the elderly who remember the distant past more clearly than the events of the previous day, Sammar lived with a young Tarig inside her head.

'When he was fourteen,' she said to Rae, 'Tarig broke his leg. He fell off a ladder while he was trying to hang up a poster in his room. The ladder fell too. It made a terrible bang which woke Mahasen from her afternoon nap. She came rushing into the room and beat him with her slipper for being careless and for waking her up. I was laughing at him, I couldn't help it. I covered my mouth knowing it was wrong to laugh when grown-ups were angry. But I couldn't stop myself. He looked so funny tangled up with the ladder, fending off Mahasen's slipper. It was a good thing she did not see me laughing or else she would have turned on me too.'

In the Winter Gardens, Sammar started to laugh. 'I always laugh,' she said, 'when people fall down, I can't help myself.' And Rae laughed and said, 'Not a very refined sense of humour.'

She said, 'No, not very,' and went on. 'His father had to take him to Germany for an operation – the doctors had to put metal pins in his calf. The day they came back, the house was full of people and all the lights were on. From Germany, they brought with them boxes and boxes of lovely chocolates. Mahasen saved

24

them for the important guests and everyone else got Mackintosh toffees, a tin that was past its sell-by date. They sold them like that, imported at the Duty Free Shop, the chocolates ashy-grey, the toffees stuck to their wrapping.

'Tarig came back different, like he was suddenly older, even though he had been away only for a month. His leg was in plaster and he had crutches which Hanan and I took turns to hop with around the house. I wrote my name in Arabic and in English on the white plaster.'

It had been easy to talk when they were young. Things changed when they outgrew sparklers and bikes. Or even, she sometimes thought, things changed from the time he broke his leg. If Hanan was with them they could talk, the three of them, about films they had seen or who Tarig had met in the petrol queue. But if Hanan left them alone, to make Tang or answer the telephone there would be an awkward silence between them. Silly talk, while they heard her stir the orange powder in the glasses, bang the ice tray in the kitchen sink. 'How are you?' 'I'm fine, how are you?' When his sister came back they would look guilty as if they had done something wrong.

Shyness pestered them for years. It was scratchy like wool. It made them want Hanan to be with them so they could talk and wanted her away from them so they could be alone. Tarig sent her notes at school with his best friend's sister, overriding Hanan, although she was in the same class. The treachery dazzled more than the words he wrote. Flimsy papers that weighed in her hand like rocks. She tore them and scattered the tiny pieces in different places, afraid that someone would find them. She liked to talk to him on the phone, it was safe on the phone. On the phone, they swapped recurrent nightmares and happy dreams. He said, 'I want to tell you something but I'm too shy.'

She imagined that what she wanted from life was simple, nothing grand, just to continue and live in the same place, be another Mahasen when she grew up. Have babies, get fat, sit with one leg crossed over the other and complain to life-long friends about the horrific rise in prices, the hours Tarig had to spend at the clinic. But continuity, it seemed, was in itself ambitious. Tarig was plucked from this world without warning, without being ill, like a little facial hair is pulled out by tweezers.

'You must tell me about this,' she said to Rae, holding up her folder. 'Are all the rumours about you true?'

'What rumours?'

'You and the terrorists or is it all top secret?'

He laughed and put his finger on the blue folder. 'You tell me first what you thought of it.'

'It's sad,' she said.

'Sad?'

'There is something pathetic about the spelling mistakes, the stains on the paper, in spite of the bravado. There are truths but they are detached, not tied to reality . . .'

'They are all like that.'

'You get a sense of people overwhelmed,' she went on, 'overwhelmed by thinking that nothing should be what it is now.'

'They are shooting themselves in the foot. There is no recourse in the Sharia for what they're doing, however much they try and justify themselves.'

'When are you going to meet them?'

He shook his head. 'I didn't get the job, they took someone else, someone with more palatable views, no doubt.'

'I am sorry about that.' She wished she had not joked about it before.

'I am sorry too. A winter in Egypt seemed to me like a good idea.' He looked at the windows. Beyond the Winter Gardens, Sammar saw a world dim with inevitable rain, metallic blue, dull green. Lawns empty of people, covered with dead leaves.

'But really it would have been good for the department. We have to prove ourselves useful to industry or the government to keep the funding coming in.'

She looked at the slabs on the ground, hexagonals by lines of pebbles. Tidy, rubbish free. Was it Tarig who always shaped designs in the dust with his feet? Or was it she? Shifted twigs, dented bottle tops, kicked around a pebble that stood out from among the rest because of its striking shape, its different colour. And to avoid Tarig's eyes, she had pulled little oblong leaves from their stems, tied the stems in knot after knot. Rolled the petals of jasmines between her fingers till they became pulp.

'I was thinking of you.' Rae said. 'This is why I wanted you to translate this. They need a translator. I would be happy to recommend you. It would be a short contract, no more than a month. Then maybe from Cairo you could go home to Khartoum for a visit. How far is it from Cairo?'

'Two and a half hours by plane.' She looked at him warily, there was now a distance between them, a new coolness. 'You imagine that I can interview terrorists?' Her voice sounded a little sarcastic, grudging.

'The place will be swarming with security. You needn't worry about that. Anyway, a lot of them would not have taken part in terrorist activities. And you're translating, not interviewing, someone else will be asking the questions. I think you'll do fine.

'These anti-terrorist programmes,' he said, 'I see them as part of a hype to cover up the real problems of unemployment and inefficient government. I've spoken to members of these extremist groups before and you will see that if you speak to them, they have no realistic policies, no clear idea of how to implement what they vaguely call "Islamic economics", or an "Islamic" state. They are protest movements, and they do have plenty to protest about. Israel's occupation of the West Bank, the mediocrity of the ruling party which has no mass support and which are in the main client states to the West. These groups appeal to people's anger, anger against class divisions, but do people really believe them to be a viable alternative? I don't think so.

'I'll get off my soap-box now,' he said and laughed. His laugh turned into a cough. 'I'm sorry to go on about this. Consider it though. I think it would be a good chance for you to go home, see your family.'

'I'm afraid.'

But he did not understand. 'It's natural to be afraid of a new job.'

When she did not answer, he said, 'There are other rooms in these gardens, do you want to see them?'

They walked away from the cacti through greenery, among tropical plants with large leaves, pink flowers. Miniature waterfalls and streams where little girls teased the swimming fish. And all around them the sound of the birds and running water. Water rushing in the pipes that ran along the ceiling to keep the air humid or was it already pouring with rain outside?

In the farthest corner, in a stagnant pond, near the toilets and the fire exit, a comical mechanised frog rose and fell. It broke the surface of the scum and rose, jaws wide open, to spit out the water it existed in. Down again it sank, heaved, only to obey and rise again. The boy with the jacket around his waist was there, kneeling by the side of the pond. He had a friend with him and they appeared to be greatly amused by the frog. The boy pulled a piece of gum out of his mouth, long and silvery, he made a loop of it and put the other end into his mouth. It dangled long, nearly touching the ground where he knelt. The actions that make mothers scold, 'Put that gum back in your mouth. Don't play with it.' She had said to Mahasen, 'I want to get married again, I need a focus in my life,' and her aunt's reply was, *Your son is your focus*. But she had left him behind, come here and her focus became the hospital room, watching from the window people doing what she couldn't do. Four years' convalescing. If she went home now, she would bring

Amir back with her, if he would agree to come. She would not escape from him again.

Glass corridors led on to other rooms where there were tree barks, plants for sale in flower pots, giant mushrooms shaped out of stone. Back in the desert room, their bench was empty, the light welcomed her. No electric frog, no foliage, just the coarse, sparse aridity that was familiar to her from long ago.

The sound of running water was the rain against the glass. It was like the rain of her dream, her first dream of the present, the first time this grey landscape had found a place in her sleeping mind. Four years and her soul had dived into the past, nothing in the present could touch it. 'But if you go home,' Rae said, 'you would find it hard to come back and I would not have a translator any more.' She learnt, then, the meaning of his kindness. That he knew she was heavy with other loyalties, full to the brim with distant places, voices in a language that was not his own.

4

Christmas Day and everything was closed, shops, work, and the bus did not pass underneath the window of her flat. No snow, the pavements black with rain. A brief day, cold silver sandwiched between two nights. Empty streets, as if people were indoors asleep or the whole day was an extended dawn of a morning that would not start until the New Year. But Sammar knew that this was not true. Somewhere hidden away was the culmination of the serious shopping of the past weeks, trees, turkeys, families sitting on settees. Like in the pictures she had seen in magazines. Private people, she thought, made private by the cold. Celebrating indoors and the streets, instead of looking festive, look bleak without people.

She could hear the television from the flat downstairs. Lesley's flat on the ground floor. The elderly lady turned it up because she could not hear so well now. Through the floorboards came applause and music, unique television sounds – the only thing not on holiday today. They kept Sammar company as the sounds of Lesley's comings and goings usually did, more so than the other tenants. The front door opening and shutting, Lesley shaking out her umbrella on the mat. She was a war widow, living alone, robust small frame, unblemished white hair, friendly and alert.

Sammar had addressed her as Aunt once out of politeness, in the early days when she had come smarting and feverish from Khartoum, without Tarig, without Amir, only the grudge against her aunt. But otherwise a soft heart, too soft, sickly soft, so that when the elderly woman had replied, taken aback, 'I'm not your aunt,' all surprise in her tired hazel eyes, 'Call me Lesley,' Sammar cried from the landing to the first floor, silly, easy tears. Surface tears like the ones chopping onions produce, even though she had not been able to cry over her son's head when she held him goodbye.

At three o'clock, when the day began to darken, she put the lights off so she could still look out of the window and not be seen. She drew loops through the condensation that clung to the glass panes, pushed with her finger drops that dribbled to the sill below. Could she trance herself to hear the azan? The sunset azan, almost as special as the dawn, when the muezzin added the words *Prayer is better than sleep*. She was fasting today, making up for days missed in Ramadan. It was easy to fast from the dawn at seven in the morning to the sunset at half-past three. Tarig would have joked about that. 'Cheating,' he would have said. 'Too easy, it doesn't count.' She remembered him fasting Ramadan when he was twelve and still going swimming, riding his bicycle in the burning heat of the afternoon, defiant and a little crazy, wanting to prove he was strong. But they had all been like that, even the girls. Are you fasting? A cool Yeah, or just a nod, deliberately casual, like it was not a big thing. Though later in the month they would copy their mothers, my head aches, I can't bear it. I have lost weight, I can hardly eat at night.

Now a little past three and Sammar counted, twenty minutes to go. She had a sheet of paper from the mosque with the times of prayer for each day. December 25th, maghrib was 15:31. She would eat a date first, drink water, pray, and then she would eat the rice she had made earlier, the rest of the beans she had cooked yesterday. Then she could spend the evening working for she had a lot of work to finish, before she went away.

She was going away in February to Egypt, part of the anti-terrorist programme. She had been to the interview in London and seen in the file that the interviewer held before him, her completed application form, photocopies of her degree, Rae's signature on the letter of reference. And she had answered all the questions confidently, as if she were strong, as if she were not afraid. At the back of her mind, the motivation, I will see home again. The job was for three weeks in which experts were going to interview members of extremist groups in Egypt and she was going to be the interpreter. After the three weeks were over, she would fly the two hours home, to Khartoum, and she would bring Amir back with her. All this needed organising, planning a new phase in her life. But the energy came, the recovery in limbs and parts of the mind that had not been used for a long time.

She had lived four years as if home had been taken away from her in the same way Tarig had. To see home again. It was a chandelier on the ceiling of her life, circles of lights. To see again the streets where Tarig had ridden his bike, and she had walked every day after school to him and Hanan, walking towards the airport, with her back to where the sun would later set. To go to where everything happened, her aunt's house; laughter on their wedding, fire when she brought Tarig's body home. Shimmering things. Painting with ice on the liver-red tiles, fearing stray dogs, in weddings dreaming of her own future wedding, visiting fortune-tellers who threw shells on the dust and never answered the questions she was there to ask.

The sound of the television fell to a quiet, even murmur. The Queen's Speech. Sammar thought that Rae would be listening to it now in Edinburgh, with his family, after the Christmas lunch in a room of red and green, in a scene like the ones she had seen in the fat catalogues that were pushed through the letter box for free. It would mean something to him, what his Queen said or did not say, in comparison to previous years. Sammar felt separate from him, exiled while he was in his homeland, fasting while he was eating turkey and drinking wine. They lived in worlds divided by simple facts – religion, country of origin, race – data that fills forms. But he doesn't drink anymore, she reminded herself. He had told her that and it had been another thing which made him less threatening. Another thing which made him not so different from her. From the beginning she had thought that he was not one of them, not modern like them, not impatient like them. He talked to her as if she had not lost anything, as if she were the same Sammar of a past time. Talked to her in that way not once, not twice, but every time. So that she had been tempted to ask, in the moments when the mind loops and ebbs, where do you know me from, why are you different from everyone else. Tempted to say, I am not strong enough for this. It had been too much visiting him that day with Yasmin. Even the day at the Winter Gardens she had gone home with the blindness coming on suddenly, blurring out bits of the granite buildings and the cars on the road.

But in February she was going home, and she could change her plans, stay there forever and he would become a memory of someone who had once been kind to her. She would remember his timetable, lectures, tutorials, the names of the Ph.D. students whose theses he supervised. An earnest man from Sierra Leone, a lady from Algeria struggling with English, two English students who wore large glasses and took the tutorials for some of his classes. Sammar liked talking to them. Over lunches and coffees in the noisy University self-service, she would move the conversation towards him. Smile as they praised him or made fun of the way he always said, 'And why is that?' The words of the students took on a lyrical quality, to be hived away, to be memorised for no reason.

At home among people she had known all her life, she would remember things she had come to know about him. The names of books lined up on the wall of his office, *How Europe Underdeveloped Africa, The Wretched of the Earth, Religion in the Third World, Culture and Imperialism, Radical Islam, Terrorism in Africa, Muslim Extremism in Egypt.*

She knew the different ways that he talked. Guarded, very careful when she asked him where he got this document of *Al-Nidaa*. 'I have friends.' Smiling, almost smug, as he held the stained papers in his hand and said, 'Researchers would kill for something as grass-roots as this!' And his voice once on the radio, on a discussion-type programme, speaking with a nervousness and urgency that was not familiar to her, '. . . not the biggest threat facing the Western world. If we look at real terrorist damage, Muslim extremists have caused much less of it than the IRA, the Red Brigade, the Baader-Meinhof gang, the Basque separatist ETA . . .'

A shift after the Winter Gardens. At the end of a long, full day when she knocked at the door of his office and he pushed back his chair. '*You* I always have time for, I can't bear anyone else at this moment except you.' Lecturing her, 'A so-called developing country is characterised by three things: one, an export-based economy; two, an inadequate infrastructure; three, a history of colonial rule.'

She knew about his asthma. Intrinsic, not triggered by an allergy. He would take two puffs of Ventolin from a blue inhaler. Shaking it first, casually while talking about something else. It left a line of powder on his lips which he licked away. The rasping sound his chest made, when she listened closely enough. He looked tired at the end of the day. Tired and coughing as winter drew in with its germs, coughing and apologising. Excuse me, Sammar, Sorry, Sammar, until her own chest hurt.

A shift after the Winter Gardens. He asked her to have her lunch with him, in his office with the glass-panelled wall through which the coffee-scented secretaries scribbled Christmas cards and Yasmin, pregnancy visible now, stared at Sammar. He was quite proud of his lunch, carefully prepared. Tuna sandwich, malted bread, two apples, four oat-bran biscuits, a can of Irn-bru. In a cold rush of intimidation, Sammar thought, is this what he does every morning, prepares his lunchbox with care. Her sandwich, smeared only with butter, was wrapped up in the same clingfilm as the day before – she could barely manage to drag herself to work in the morning darkness. And, horror, it was true, there was a green furry spot on the edge of the bread she was holding in her hands. Stinging shame, mouldy sandwich. Clumsy exit, days of avoiding him, avoiding Yasmin. Only listening to his students praise him; lyrics from Sierra Leone, in Arabic from the Algerian lady.

She turned on the tap and the gush drowned the sound of Lesley's TV. Of all the people in the building, Sammar saw Lesley the most. Lesley was the one who answered the telephone in the landing, a pay-phone shared by everyone except Lesley, who had her own portable telephone with answering machine (won as a prize from the Littlewoods catalogue). When Sammar and Lesley spoke they spoke of the weather or Lesley complained about the other tenants. The students who quarrelled and one of them called the police, 'what a carry on'; and how the girl in 3b ended up in Casualty when she covered herself in cooking oil and lay in the sun of a heatwave July. Lesley was always busy, she went out in every kind of weather to play Bingo. In the months when Sammar had hauled her pain up and down the stairs, she would admire Lesley, so many years older than herself and more full of life. Living alone and filling up with her own self the empty space of a flat, a garden, a niche in life.

Thirty-five minutes past three and Sammar ate a date that tasted even sweeter because she was breaking a fast. Then she drank the water and felt herself to be simple, someone with a simple need, easily fulfilled, easily granted. The dates and the water made her heart feel big, with no hankering or tanginess or grief.

She rinsed her hands. Her wet face in the mirror was not different from the Sammar of the past, softer perhaps, blurred, the eyes dimmer than they had been. She rinsed her feet. Yesterday she had noticed her feet, noticed their dryness and cared enough to buy a pumice stone. She had scraped the rough skin that had not been removed for years. She had also noticed her hair, put unsalted butter on it like she had done before, wrapped it in silver foil and felt the butter melt through her scalp before she shampooed it away. Her hair will become stronger that way, shiny after the years of neglect, the strands of white that Tarig had not seen.

Her prayer mat had tassels on the edges, a velvety feel, a smell that she liked. The only stability in life, unreliable life, taking turns the mind could not imagine. When she finished praying, she sat for the *tasbeeh,* her thumb counting on each segment of her fingers, three for each finger, fifteen for a hand, *Astaghfir Allah, Astaghfir Allah, Astaghfir Allah, . . . I seek forgiveness from Allah . . . I seek forgiveness from Allah . . . I seek forgiveness . . .* the twenty-ninth time, thirty, she heard the telephone in the landing ring, thirty-one, thirty-two, Lesley's footsteps on the stairs, thirty-three, and what was left of her concentration scattered with the knock on the door.

His voice sounded complaining, the first greeting, her name and she felt herself tugged away from the day that had been unrolling upstairs. He said, 'It's Rae here,' as he always did at work on the telephone. She was slow in replying, wondering why he was calling her on a holiday, from another city. He asked, 'Were you asleep?' and this made her laugh, warm towards him, he who was able to imagine a siesta in the darkness of a British Christmas afternoon.

'I finally managed to get hold of that Azhar thesis I was telling you about,' he said. She remembered him mentioning it, the topic was about justice and the ruler or the unjust ruler, she was not sure.

'That's good,' she said. 'It's been difficult to get hold of?'

'Slow. But I'm very pleased now.' He did not sound pleased, though, his voice sounded strained. 'We'll meet when I get back. Maybe you could start translating the abstract and the title chapters, the introduction perhaps. You're leaving soon, you won't have much time.'

'Six weeks,' she said, 'about six weeks.'

'You're counting the days?'

'Sometimes. I think I will have time to do the introduction too, if it's not very long.'

'We'll see when I get back and show it to you,' he said. She expected him to end the conversation, say goodbye. She did not expect the silence that followed.

'Are you enjoying the holiday?' she asked.

'No, not enjoying it. There is too much talk of food in this house. They are food connoisseurs here. They eat and at the same time talk of other meals, reminisce about dishes. Over breakfast they're planning what they'll cook for dinner, arguing about it.'

'They,' Sammar learned, were his ex-wife's family. He was staying with them because his daughter, Mhairi, was there. She spent the school holidays in her grandparents home. Her mother was still in Geneva, where she worked with the WHO.

Culture-shock for Sammar. An old man in Edinburgh was allowing his daughter's ex-husband under his roof. This must be civilised behaviour, an 'amicable divorce'. Where she come from, the divorced spouse was one who 'turned out to be a son of a dog' or 'she turned out to be mad' and were treated as such. No one 'stayed friends', no one stayed on talking terms.

She asked about his daughter. He said that she was pretty and saturated today with Christmas presents. He said that every time he saw her, it took a day or two for her to speak to him beyond yes, no and don't know, then she talked non-stop until she got on his nerves. He said that everyday so far, except today, they had escaped from the *cordon bleu* of the house to the glaring yellow of Burger King and a Kebab take-away shop. He said that he wanted Mhairi to grow up to be as subversive as him.

About his ex-wife's parents and the food, Sammar said, 'Maybe they want you to get back together again and so they are being extra hospitable.'

Nothing she said startled him. She was almost used to this now.

'No, it's not like that. They're quite satisfied with the way things are.' He went on in an even voice, 'When you are climbing the WHO's ladder of success, the last thing you need is a husband skulking around, criticising the UN, pointing out the hypocrisy of their policies.'

Sammar held the receiver tight and stared at the bicycles that were stored under the staircase, the 'Don't Forget Your Keys' sign on the front door.

'On the day before I came here,' he said, 'I was down in Personnel and I needed to photocopy something. The photocopier was in a small room that I had never been into before. It had old curtains in a large pattern of orange and brown. A kind of distinctive seventies' look, out-dated now. They made me remember the house. We had curtains like these, bright orange, blue and brown. It was a good house – built in the late sixties, with a view over the Dee. The kitchen and lounge were upstairs and there were windows from floor to ceiling along the whole length of the room. All for the brilliant view. It would remind you of the Nile, Sammar, only the Nile is wider and its banks less complex. It reminded me of the Nile. We were just back from Egypt then. She had not liked it there much. She liked walking and Cairo is not a city for walks.

'I remember when the house got sold, she came from Geneva to pack. I would come home from work and find her sitting on the floor smoking and sorting out things. Too many things. Books and records, old clothes. We never liked throwing things away, magazines, newspapers, they would just pile up. I taped the boxes and she divided everything up. She left me everything that was North African, everything Islamic.

'We used to smoke together when we first met. Cigarettes and other things. It was the thing to do then. She smoked even through her pregnancy. I only stopped when my asthma got worst. But still the house was full of smoke, cigarette smoke and bad feelings.'

Sammar could see a house with orange curtains, a river view, rooms filled with beautiful objects, European and African things. Inside the house life was smoke and bad feelings.

'At night,' he said, 'quarrels . . . I used to feel such peace when I went to work in the morning, talked to the students, soothed myself with a lecture on Foreign Policy Analysis. I stayed late, avoided going home. And the later I went home, the later the quarrelling started, the later it went on through the night. Sleep deprivation is torture. I used to dose off while driving. I fell asleep once, while she was talking, I just fell asleep, I felt like I was drugged. She shook me awake, saying "Listen, listen to me" . . .,' he started to cough. He coughed until Sammar's heart hurt. The landing was cold. Through Lesley's door she heard the piano music of a comedy show.

'You're ill?' she said.

'I'm coming down with something, yes.'

Sammar changed the receiver from one hand to another and wiped her palm against her jumper. She wanted him to keep talking, keep talking until her ears were flattened and bruised.

'I'm sorry, I'm talking too much,' he said.

'No.' She searched for something to say, something appropriate, sympathetic. He had talked to her suddenly so personally and all she had managed to say was 'You're ill?'

She began to speak about work. It made her feel more confident.

'I found a translation of the Qudsi Hadiths. On alternate pages they have them in English and Arabic. There is also a good introduction on how they differ from the Qur'an.'

'What do they say? How do they put it?'

She was not prepared for that and faltered a little, saying that the book was upstairs and she would have to get it and would his hosts not mind that he was on the telephone for so long.

'Don't worry about them,' he said, 'they're very organized. Their bills come itemized. I've had to call overseas before, Egypt and Morocco and I settle it with them later.' His voice sounded lighter than before.

She ran up the stairs that she had often taken a step at a time, dragging her grief. Now the staircase had a different aura, a different light and it was just her and Lesley alone in the whole building. The other tenants were away for the holidays and the stairs belonged to her alone. Where was she now, which country? What year? She climbed the stairs into a hallucination in which the world had swung around. Home and the past had come here and balanced just for her. The stairs in a warm yellow light and sounds of a party, people talking and someone laughed. She was inside the laughter, wearing something new, carrying a tray, mindful of the children who swirled and dived around her knees. She offered glasses of something that was dark and sweet, and when someone refused, coaxed them until they changed their minds. Someone called her name, she had to hurry, look over her shoulder, locate the voice, shout back, I'm coming now.

She sat on the floor of the landing and read out, over the phone, the notes she had made from the book. 'A definition given by the scholar al-Jurjani, "A Sacred Hadith is, as to its meaning, from Allah the Almighty; as to the wording, it is from the Messenger of Allah, peace be upon him. It is that which Allah the Almighty has communicated to His Prophet through revelation or in dream and he, peace be upon him, has communicated it in his own words.

Thus the Qur'an is superior to it because, besides being revealed, it is Allah's wording." In a definition given by a later scholar al-Qari, ". . . Unlike the Holy Qur'an, Sacred Hadith are not acceptable for recitation in one's prayers, they are not forbidden to be touched or read by one who is in a state of ritual impurity . . . and they are not characterized by the attribute of inimitability." '

Rae said, 'This is very clear, thank you. What about their subject matter? I would imagine they do not cover legislation . . .'

'Yes, generally not. There is a section on their subject matter.' She turned the pages of the book, '. . . they clarify the meanings of the Divinity . . . the style takes the form of usually direct expression . . . I'll read you one of them. The Prophet, peace be upon him said, *"Allah Almighty says: I am as My servant thinks I am. I am with him when he makes mention of Me. If he makes mention of Me to himself, I make mention of him to Myself; and if he makes mention of Me in an assembly, I make mention of him in a better assembly. And if he draws near to Me a hand's span, I draw near to him an arm's length; and if he draws near to Me an arm's length, I draw near to him a fathom's length. And if he comes to Me walking, I go to him at speed."* '

Rae was slow in replying. 'Would you have translated it in exactly the same way?'

'For the first sentence, there is a footnote which says, another possible rendering of the Arabic is, *I am as My servant expects Me to be.* And I feel this is closer to the Arabic word which means expects, thinks, even speculates.'

'In this society,' he said, 'in this secular society, the speculation is that God is out playing golf. With few exceptions and apart from those who are self-convinced atheists, the speculation is that God has put up this elaborate solar system and left it to run itself. It does not need Him to maintain it or sustain it in anyway. Mankind is self-sufficient . . .'

'But why golf?' she asked. 'Why specifically golf?' And he laughed for the first time that day.

5

On Boxing Day and the weekend that followed and on Hogmanay, before the streets filled again with cars and schoolchildren, before the other tenants came back from their holidays, Sammar waited by the landing armed against the cold: layers of wool, socks, a cushion to sit on, barrier against the floorboards. The awkward time was the ringing of the telephone, the harsh sound of it and knowing that the call was for her, knowing who it would be. The first sentences were awkward too. Her name. Hello. The weather: snowing in Edinburgh. Frosty in Aberdeen, freezing.

'How are you?'

'How are you? How is Mhairi?'

'What are you taking for your cold?'

He said that he'd read in the papers that thousands went abroad that time of year, in search of skiing or the sun. The popular destinations were the ski slopes of France or Tenerife. He said, 'This is the best time of year for Morocco, Libya, the Middle East.' Rae remembered a train ride in the seventies, from Tangiers south, to Marrakesh. Rain and then the sun came out into the crowded train. A man with a large moustache offered him a cigarette and they talked about the raid on Entebbe. Rae remembered a time when he could breathe like other people, when there was more air in the world.

She said, 'We have a winter in Sudan, a cold that stays on the skin, does not punch inside to the bones, is content to crack people's skin, turn it into the colour of ash.' She said that the cold hurt when she was young and remembered the pouring of glycerin, burning, being told, don't lick it off, don't lick it off your lips. Or tasteless Vaseline, in plastic tubs, with grains of sand, brown and coarse in the thick silver mess. Or Nivea cream, the blue tin of luxury that came with a German ad on TV.

He asked her, 'Which is bluer: the Nile or Nivea tins?'

She said that colours made her sad. Yellow as she knew it and green as she knew it were not here, not bright, not vivid as they should be. She had stacked the differences; the weather, the culture, modernity, the language, the silence of the muezzin, then found that the colours of mud, sky and leaves, were different too.

He said, his voice changed by flu, 'The Nile is bluer. Did you not look at it, did you instead watch *Peyton Place* on TV? I ask because in the West Bank, the children threw stones at the soldiers in the mornings and watched *Dallas* at night sitting together on the floor.'

She said, 'At night we used to sleep outdoors. We used to pull our beds out at sunset, so that the sheets would be cool later. It was so hot that sheets taken out of a cupboard, spread out to lie on were too unpleasant, they had to be cooled first. Every night, I saw bats in the clouds and the grey blur of a bird. And around the moon was another light, always the same shape. In the distant past, Muslim doctors advised nervous people to look up at the sky. Forget the tight earth. Imagine that the sky, all of it, belonged to them alone. Crescent, low moon, more stars than the eyes looking up at them. But the sky was free, without any price, no one I knew spoke of it, no one competed for it. Instead, one by one those who could afford it began to sleep indoors in cool, air-conditioned rooms, away from the mosquitoes and the flies, away from the azan at dawn. Now when they build houses, when they build apartment blocks, they don't build them with places for people to sleep outdoors. It is a thing of the past, something I remember from my past.'

He said, 'This is the enemy, what is irreversible, what has already reached the farthest of places. There is no going back. They can bomb bus-loads of tourists, burn the American flag, but they are not shooting the enemy. It is already with them, inside them, what makes them resentful, defensive, what makes them no longer confident of their vision of the world.'

She thought about that, he made her think. The landing existed with the bicycles under the stairs and the winter sun seeping through the edges of the letter box. But all that was unreal, superseded. What was real was that she had been given permission to think and talk, and he would not be surprised by anything she said. As if he had given her a promise, never to be taken aback. Surprise was part of the city, the granite buildings, the buses that went down the narrowest of roads. There were shades of surprise: surprise-sneer, surprise-embarrassed, surprise-bemused, surprise-disapproving. She had to be silent. Use her teeth and lips to keep silent.

Now the rules were being broken. They broke when she said, in Rae's flat, her fingers on the magazine, 'I used to wear a uniform like that in school.' The rules broke and burst her head in little bright pieces.

First African night. She spoke first, for like him she was born in this wintery kingdom. Like him Africa was arrived at and loved.

They came from London at night. A father with a successful degree, a mother who had given birth to her children abroad, a seven-year-old Sammar. It was her first time on an airplane, that was her excitement in the weeks before, not where she was going. Home was a vague place, a jumble of what her mother said. Home was a grey and white place like in the photographs of her cousins which arrived air mail. It was the airplane, the airplane, in the weeks before the flight. New clothes to wear on the airplane, a doll to keep her quiet, can she sit near the window? Can she open the window? A smooth oval window. The beauty of the tray the hostess brings, the perfect cups, the plates filled with different things, hot, cold, different colours. Sugar in a packet, a toothpick for her to unwrap and play with, poke the eyes of the doll. Then the smallest pillow to sleep on. Can we take the pillow with us? Why not? Why not?

There were many people waiting for them in the car park of Khartoum airport. People who made a fuss and spoke at the same time. A woman burst into tears, men hugged her father, children stared at Sammar. Her cousins, Hanan and Tarig. They curiously shook her hand. Ahmed Ali Yasseen was there. He picked her up and lifted her high above the cars and the other children. She was above them all. He said, 'What did you get me from London?' 'Nothing,' she shrugged and he laughed and everyone who heard her laughed too. And she did not understand what they found funny, she was just happy to be carried, lifted up. She was at that age when she was often told, you are too old to be carried, you are too heavy, you are a big girl now.

Their luggage disappeared into different cars. Sammar and her parents were separated too in different cars, going to the same place, her aunt's house for dinner and to spend the night. Sammar rode with 'Am Ahmed in his Toyota pick-up van. She sat with his wife, in the front seat and Tarig rode in the back. He kept standing up and being told off by 'Am Ahmed, 'Sit down properly boy, or I'll bring you in front with me.' But Tarig could never be still, it was in his nature to be always jumping about, attracting attention. Sammar thought he was silly. Later as the months went by she thought him brave, brave and silly mixed up together, doing forbidden things she did not have the courage to do, like playing with the razors they found in the dust or riding their bicycles on the busy, main roads.

Her aunt's house was not far away, it was not a long drive. On the telephone Rae asked, 'How far?'

'Not far,' she replied, and moved the receiver from one hand to the other, one ear to the other, 'not far, like from Holburn Street to Old Aberdeen. And it was late at night so there was not much traffic. Khartoum is poorly lit at night. To someone not used to it, it would appear gloomy, warm and dull. When one of the street lights goes off, it's a long time before it is fixed, weeks and months. But there is no fear in the dark. The streets are safe except for the stray dogs, and the open drains, holes in the pavements through which anyone can easily fall.'

'Did you ever fall?'

'No.' She laughed and it was as if the landing was warm like the nights in Khartoum she had been describing.

In the car, she told Rae, 'Am Ahmed's wife smiled at her all the time. She had a gold tooth which Sammar tried to pull out and this made the woman laugh with her dimples and fat arms. She gave Sammar one of her gold bracelets instead. It was too big. Sammar pushed it up on to her arm, tried it on the other arm, dropped in on the floor and had to scramble down to pick it up.

Her aunt's house was full of lights. Those first garden lights would blur with other lights, party lights in the years to come, wedding lights. The cars were parked on the driveway, and on the road outside. Sammar saw her parents with her baby brother Waleed, they were now not interested in her, absorbed in the relatives and friends they had not seen for years. And though reassured that they were near, she was not interested in them either. She was too aware of everyone and everything around her. The newness of the warm night, the shabby cars, and the big house that was before her. A lighted house in front of an empty square that was covered in darkness. A square that was large and mysterious; broken glass lay on its dust, dogs barked their way through the rubbish that was dumped there. Underneath the carport, as they walked inside, Sammar showed Hanan the bracelet, let her try it on. They compared the length of their arms, the size of their wrists. A beginning. In years to come they would compare their polished nails, the hair on their arms, the lines on their palms.

Her aunt, Mahasen, was the tall woman in the sun-coloured tobe, the woman who had not come to the airport. She was part of the house, part of its lights. The woman who walked across the grass with an outstretched hand saying, 'My brother . . .,' and hugged Sammar's father first. The woman examined baby Waleed and squealed, 'He's ugly, what kind of creation is this!', and everyone laughed as she pinched his cheeks and kissed his fore-head. Mahasen sat on one of the chairs in the garden and drew Sammar to her. Sammar took in the sudden perfume, the flowers embroidered on the sun-coloured tobe, its texture so close. Mahasen smoothed Sammar's eyebrows with her thumb, touched her earlobes, her chin. 'This is the one who pleases me,' she said, with a laugh to her brother. And she stood up, so tall she was, so much embroidered and bright folds. 'Come with me, Sammar.'

She held her aunt's hand. Elegant hands that never washed dishes, never scrubbed floors. Inside the house, the floor was all speckled tiles, brown and black speckles, an imitation of marble. A huge expanse of hard, square tiles. Strange for Sammar. She was used to the unobtrusive carpets and wood of London's flats. These tiles were for counting, for sliding across. Her aunt's high-heeled sandals made a tapping noise on the tiles. Yellow sandals to match the tobe, red-brick toenails, heels that were regularly sloughed, daily massaged with cream. Her aunt's bedroom had a large mirror, jars of lotions and creams. A transistor radio, a painting of gazelles, a huge bed with blue pillows. And on the side-table was what her aunt had brought her to see. A photograph of a girl feeding pigeons. The pigeons swarmed near her outstretched hands, one was perched on her frightened shoulder. The stone lion of Trafalger Square loomed above. 'This is me!' Sammar said. The first words she spoke in her aunt's house.

'That night,' she said to Rae on the telephone, 'that night like nearly every night, the grown-ups sat in the garden. When I got older I was allowed to sit with them, on seats with cool cushions and above us all the stars. Insects attacked the garden lights, those that got too close became black dots sticking to the hot glass. The garden was filled with sounds: laughter and loud narratives, the ceaseless croaking of frogs, the softer sounds of grasshoppers. And from the square, the stray dogs howled, a sound of faraway sadness.'

On that first night in Khartoum, she wandered around the garden with Hanan and Tarig, to the back of the house where there was no garden, inside the house, upstairs to the roof and its row of empty beds. Everywhere they went, Tarig did what Hanan and Sammar would not do. In the garden he took off his sandals and walked in the mud of the flower beds. He tore the leaves off the eucalyptus tree. There was a swing in the far corner of the garden. He swung on it standing up and when he was very high, he jumped off, effortlessly, without fear.

At the back of the house was the smell of flames and marinated lamb. The cook grilled kebabs on a coal fire. He wore a *jellabia* and his eyes were red. He sat on a small stool and fanned the flames with a newspaper. Tarig squatted next to him, and reached out for a piece of meat. The cook hit him with the newspaper over his head, 'Get away, you'll burn yourself.' But Tarig laughed, ducked from another blow and grabbed a piece of meat, grey, still barely cooked. And he disgusted them all by chewing and chewing on the piece of meat and then spitting it away. 'My brother is horrible,' Hanan said to Sammar. 'I hate him.' Sammar was distracted by Tarig, her eyes fixed on him. She liked her cousin Hanan better.

On the roof, they looked down over the railings at their parents below. They were sitting in a large circle, they never looked up. Some of the men were smoking and their cigarettes made pretty little red lights that moved from side to side. On the roof the sky was bigger than the house and the square. The darkness was speckled with stars, speckled like the house's tiles, except that the sky's speckles were not still. Suddenly, a large grey shadow climbed through the transparent clouds, blinking red lights, a deep roar. 'That's your airplane,' Tarig said, looking up. He had been leaning too far over the rail. Now he swung back, his hands clutching the top of the rail, his whole weight carried by his arms. 'Our airplane?' Sammar didn't understand. 'It's the airplane you came on,' he said, 'it's going back to London without you.'

On the telephone, Rae coughed, 'Sorry. Excuse me Sammar.' He put the receiver down to blow his nose, clear his throat, spit into a handkerchief. She could hear him.

They talked about her father and aunt, how fast things change in that part of the world. He asked her questions. 'And why is that?' he asked. After she answered he was silent, as if he was thinking about what she had said. She imagined him wiping his face with his hand.

They talked about Khartoum. Khartoum, where the Blue and the White Niles met under the bridge, under the sun, and across the bridge Umdurman, where saints were buried and something old and whole was in the air. Above the sand and the sound of the wind, everything held together, connected. He knew the details of her country's history more than she did, the correct dates. They both knew the names . . . the Mahdi, Gordon, the Khalifa, Kitchener and Wingate.

'There is a statue,' said Rae, 'of Gordon in Aberdeen. In Schoolhill. Have you see it?'

'No.' She did not see much, she walked around asleep.

'You might like to look at it sometime.' A plaque in stone, the words *died in Khartoum 1885*.

'I didn't know he was Scottish. They didn't teach us that at school.'

'It was the British . . .'

'The *Ingeleez* . . .' They laughed and the wind rattled the front door a little and passed.

He said that he had never been to Khartoum. There were plans once but they did not materialise. She said, 'I wish you would see it. It's beautiful . . .' and paused, wanting to say more, to describe in words: simple, authentic, subservient to nature. Her voice was sad when she said, 'But it is not considered beautiful . . .'

'By who?'

'People who know the world more than me.'

'But I trust you,' he said. 'You make me feel safe. I feel safe when I talk to you.' She picked up the word 'safe' and put it aside, to peel it later and wonder what it meant. Sitting on the floor of the landing, she thought that this was a miracle. Not only his voice, but that happiness could come here at the foot of the stairs, the same stairs that were, once, so difficult to climb, that led to her room of hibernation, the hospital room.

6

On New Year's Day, on the weekend that followed, Sammar sat at the foot of the stairs, listening to Rae. On the telephone he talked about a first night in Morocco and images come to her of a place she had never been. A decade when she was a girl and he was an adult.

The plan was that the three of them would drive the van from Edinburgh down to France, Spain, then cross the Mediterranean at Algeciras by boat to Tangiers. Rae, Steve and Chris, early twenties in the late sixties, just through with university, ready for the dope trail, ready for the dark continent. Chris wanted to drift, to break away from what, he didn't know. He lifted weights and hated himself. While driving he blew impatiently and ruffled the long fringe that fell over his eyes. Steve kept the peace, believed in friendship and love, was one of the few people that Chris didn't hate. Steve wanted to go to India, North Africa was a compromise for him, a gracious accession to the wishes of the other two.

In the van Rae rambled on about *The Republic* and *Das Kapital*, about Livingstone, about Richard Burton, the African explorer and translator of the Arabian Nights. About a long-lost Uncle David he had in Egypt, African cousins. Names that he knew, as cities and towns passed by, Fidel Castro, Golda Meir, Haile Selassie, Franz Fanon and the anti-colonial struggle.

'My hero Malcolm X, I heard that man speak at the LSE, I went down . . . the way he gripped the audience . . .'

'Shut it, will you!'

'Shut up!'

He would not shut up. It took him years to learn the value of silence, the power of carefully chosen words. That summer his voice went on and on, a steady monotone as the van made its way through England, through the countryside of France, the sunshine of Spain. When it was his turn to drive, he talked less but it was not often his turn to drive. Chris liked to be the one driving, being a passenger bored him. Rae only shut up completely when he was reading or listening to his crackling transistor radio which was tuned to the World Service. He listened intently, oblivious to his surroundings. Things were happening around the world, historical events. He kept quiet also in the rare company of girls. Girls liked Steve, he had the looks, he played the guitar. Chris did stupid things when girls were around like kicking the tyres of the van, revving the engine when they gave two Parisian hitch-hikers a ride. For Chris life was a rubber band wound tight around him. He bickered with Rae all the way. And Rae goaded and teased him, gave him lectures from the back seat of the van, surrounded by the luggage, the radio, Steve's guitar.

'The Highlands were the first place the English colonised . . .'

'Enough, Rae.'

'. . . later India and Africa. They got Scottish men to pillage that place for the Empire. It was Scottish men who lost their lives . . .'

'Shut up, will you.'

'They were the foot soldiers. The ones the spears got first, the spears of the dervishes and the Fuzzy-Wuzzies. Kipling called them that in a poem. Hey Music Boy! Did you hear of the Fuzzy-Wuzzies? Chris, you illiterate buffoon, you? I still insist on the notion that anyone who hasn't read Fanon deserves to be shot . . .'

Chris braked, yanked open the door of the van, got out and hauled a baffled at first and then resistant Rae on to the side of the road. The amateur weight-lifter found the resistance not difficult to overcome. It did not take long, in terms of time. The defeated Rae was left behind, by the side of the road. In the van Steve was laughing, making faces at him and gestures with his hands. To Algeciras, Rae limped the five miles, wiped the blood that trickled from his nose. He was without his precious World Service, without his books, his passport, his clothes. It was not funny. He found them waiting for him at the port. Silence was their apology. He hated them, he hated practical jokes. He could see the end coming soon, the end of this threesome. He slept in the back of the van, slept soundly while sunset and the boat floated over the Strait of Gibraltar.

Night-time and the first sight of Africa's shore. Lights along the harbour of Tangiers, around him the tune of another language, men unconcerned with his foreignness. The boat was full of Moroccan itinerant workers returning home from France and Spain, carrying sacks and plastic bags. Some with families had loaded old cars, smelly diesels, a battered red Mercedes covered in blue canvas. Singer sewing machines, irons, refrigerators, food blenders, transistor radios. They all looked in the same direction, at the lights and shadows of Tangiers under the low African sky. Rae stood with them, more in awe, more wretched than they. He felt stale and unclean, with his shirt torn and his hair covered in dust. His nose and chest burnt from the smell of the diesel. A pattern was set from that first time. In years to come every arrival to Africa was similarly accompanied by loss or pain, a blow to his pride. Baggage disappearing, nights spent in quarantine, stolen travellers' cheques. As if from him the continent demanded a forfeit, a repayment of debts from the ghosts of the past.

*   *   *

Of the years he spent in Morocco, he spoke to Sammar on the telephone from Stirling. He had by then left Edinburgh, left the house of his ex-wife's parents, said goodbye to his daughter. Sammar felt the change in his voice. It was lighter, he was more at ease. In Stirling there were cousins and an old uncle to visit in a nursing home, the elder brother of the long-lost David. 'Today,' Rae said, 'my uncle didn't recognise me at all. Last year was better. Last year he thought I was David, and we talked a bit. I liked that.'

In Stirling, there was Dr Fareed Khalifa, educationalist and UK resident for ten years. The two of them were invited by the debating society as speakers to oppose the proposition, 'This House Fears the Threat of Radical Islam'.

'I said to him, "Fareed, we're going to lose, it's almost pre-determined. They've even got a bottle of champagne as the prize for the best floor speaker, so they're not thinking it will be you. If the results are less than 80 per cent in favour of the House, then we've done well." And Sammar, that man looked devastated. He said, "You are defeatist, it's *my* faith that I am defending and I'll defend it with all I've got." '

Rae said, 'I wasn't too happy to be called defeatist.'

She told him he was being realistic not defeatist.

He said, 'I'm trying not to be defeatist about this flu. Nights are the worst, sleeping makes me feverish and I can hardly breathe lying down. I should get back to my doctor in Aberdeen.'

She said, shyly, and with pauses in the middle, 'I would not mind . . . if you call me in the middle of the night . . . if you can't sleep.' She, who had for years hibernated, could now hardly sleep. His voice during the day and the day-dreams at night. Dreaming, dreaming and not sleeping.

The first ring of the telephone through a dream of colours and people. She groped her way down the stairs, soft from sleep. Hoping the old woman would not wake up. It was two o'clock in the morning. Prayers to God Almighty that Lesley would not hear the ringing of the telephone, sleep deeply, soundly.

'Your voice is so beautiful,' he said. He was feverish and the words came out of him in a jumble. Words that went to her head became little jewels, coloured gems, precious stones to carry around.

He said that he wanted to take her to places where she would forget and remember. Show her a bend in the Dee and she would see the Nile. Show her a house with a flat roof, a lighthouse that looked like a white minaret, castles where believers lived long ago, subservient to the climate. He said, 'We could go for a drive when I get back to Aberdeen.'

She was silent. Listening to the sounds of the night, his breathing. Once upon a time, in another part of the world, were the fears *someone will see us together, alone together . . . a woman's reputation is fragile as a match stick . . . a woman's honour . . .* Reputation was the idol people set up, what determined the giving, the holding back. *A girl's honour . . . your father will kill you . . . your brother will beat you up . . .* you will go to school the next morning as the bolder girls inevitably did, with puffy red eyes, unusually subdued.

But idols' powers are not infinite. They cover a place, a particular community and a time. Sammar watched Reputation lose its muscle, its vigour, shrink and frizzle out in this remote corner of the world. When idols fall, the path to the truth is uncluttered, clear. Who saw her, knew her, was with her all the time wherever she went?

She said, 'You are right. I would like to see castles where believers lived long ago helpless and yet strong, a lighthouse tall as a minaret, a house with a flat roof like my aunt's house. But it would be wrong. I'm sorry, very sorry.'

She was afraid that he would be angry with her, impatient, bored. She bit her lips.

He said, 'Don't worry, don't say sorry. I wouldn't want you to do anything you are uncomfortable with.'

The next day he asked about her son. 'You never told me your son's name,' he said.

She said, 'He is called Amir, and it means prince.' She thought of the child, walking barefooted in the mud, throwing his toys down from the roof, like Tarig. She said to Rae, 'I worry about bringing him here. He will find it difficult at first, the weather, and all the layers of clothes he must wear.'

'Do you know how to drive?' Rae asked.

She did, long ago. 'Am Ahmed taught her, taught them all, driving around the empty square, in the hot afternoons while Mahasen slept. The memory was vivid. Clouds of dust and jumpy starts.

She laughed, 'Driving there is not like driving here. Few rules and there are easy ways of getting a licence, without a test at all.'

He knew, he understood. He said, 'It's all a bit uptight here. It has to be because of the sheer number of cars, the speed.'

Sammar thought of the way Tarig died. Cars. Speed and an elderly man blinded by the summer sun making a fatal mistake. She brooded a little. It never made sense. A gentle old man blinded by the sun, killing Tarig. An apologetic, tearful little man. The ifs were snakes, hissing, if Tarig had gone out a minute earlier, a minute later, if he had seen that old man driving towards him, if it had been a cloudy day like so many of this city's cloudy days, like so many of this city's cloudy days. The ifs were poisonous snakes, whispering. For years the ifs had tangled up her mind, tugged away at her faith, made her unable to walk up the stairs.

Rae talked about driving lessons so that she would be able to drive her son around. He talked about driving schools and driving tests. His voice came from far away, she was slipping.

'I had a son in Morocco,' he said and paused. 'Still-born . . . I think that is the right word.'

He spoke and lifted her up to see places she hadn't seen, people she would never meet. They took shape in her imagination, how they looked, how they spoke, the things Rae told her in detail, the things he left out.

He stayed behind after Chris and Steve drove back in the van. Steve still wanting India, Chris wanting England, both unfulfilled. He found a job in a craft shop, owned by a local scholar and his French wife. The shop was named after her. She had fine taste and the shop did not have a tacky, touristy feel. The expatriate community brought their souvenirs and gifts from there: foreign journalists, Westernised Moroccans, French diplomats. The owner of the shop and his wife entertained their regular customers in the shop, while Rae dealt with the casual buyers, changed the bulbs on the display window. He listened to their conversations: Palestine, what Fanon said, what Sartre said . . . Nasser closed the Straits of Tiran! . . . Six days of war, six days! . . . Israel took Sinai, the West Bank . . .

When he expressed interest, ventured an opinion, they welcomed him, listened. His employer nodding his head, puffing at his pipe, correcting him here and there on a factual error, getting him to temper his more extreme views. Surrounded by calligraphy, arabesque, what was intricately woven, what was embroidered on cloth, Rae learnt what he had not learnt in university nor in the debating society he had been so active in. Things more important than anger, more important than an argument cleverly expressed.

Of all the customers that came to the shop, foreign journalists interested him the most. He admired their knowledgeable manners, their easy coming and goings. He followed them around from one hotel bar to another, from one party to another until they yawned and told him to go home. Home was a flat he shared with three Air Maroc pilots. They were away most of the time and he was left on his own to walk barefooted on the tiles, sit out on the balcony with his transistor radio. On the rare occasions when all three pilots were in town at the same time, the flat was crowded, the atmosphere like that of a party or a souk. They were his link with the people of the city. With them he visited the cafés, played dominos, smoked the hubble-bubble pipe. He went into mosques, learnt to take his shoes off, sit cross-legged on the floor. The pilots were happy to talk about their work, their country, their religion. They introduced him to cousins and friends, lunch at an aunt's house, the wedding of a school-mate. When the pilots were away, the flat was full of Rae's thoughts and the crackling of the BBC World Service. The silver antennae of the transistor stuck out at an angle that he had spent a long time getting just right.

While the pilots were his link with the locals, his employers were the link with the international community. In small expatriate communities, social integration is as fast as the judgement passed on a newcomer. Those his age and older decided they did not like him much. He was cheeky and somewhat secretive. He did not have the straightforward charm they admired; he did not have the cool, self-determined look that they favoured. In some shadows, according to the ladies, he looked exactly like an Arab. Rae got along better with the young who had grown up in Morocco, a minority of privileged lives. He did what the young did not do: he read newspapers, he was learning Arabic. Wandering into mosques, living with Moroccans. This was subversive enough for the young ones. They liked him.

Young Amelia was lovely in her Parisian clothes which the house-boy ironed. Amelia's father was English and her mother was Spanish. Her mother was one of the best cooks around and it showed on her happy daughter. It made her look older than eighteen. 'Amelia is like Marilyn Monroe – a size sixteen,' said her proud mother to her friends, who much preferred the figures of Twiggy and Mary Quant. Amelia had not gone back to England to boarding school as her contemporaries had: she was too attached to her mother and her mother's dishes. Morocco was her home, it

was in her Spanish blood, her English spoken with a certain lilt –
her attraction for Rae.

Rae sat with Amelia as she sunbathed by the pool. Bikini from
Paris. The setting had a colonial air about it, in the Arab waiters
spotless in their white uniforms, in the cocktails served by the pool.
Leaves fell into the water and a wretched-looking man with rolled
up trousers, inferior in status to the waiters, removed the leaves
with a long net. The man, the waiters and Rae were the only ones
who were fully dressed. Rae wore khaki-green. Khaki-green and
khaki-brown were his favourite colours, his image.

In the presence of Amelia, Rae was dizzy from the sun, the
perfect blue of the pool. A clear thought wound its way through
his brain, he told Amelia about it. She narrowed her eyes, hazel
eyes with green. The waiters. The thought was about the waiters.
Their women were covered, seldom glimpsed, while they earned
their living serving iced lemonade to pool-side beauties. In the
evening they mixed cocktails, sliced lemons for the water-coloured
gin, poured whisky, when alcohol was forbidden to them. That
was why, Rae said to Amelia, they had shifty eyes, pathetic giggles,
why they went home everyday and beat their children up.

Part of Amelia's charm was her parents muted disapproval of
him. In an evening party by that same pool, a band played 'Nights
in White Satin', and Rae danced with Amelia while her parents
patiently glowered. He was in love, abroad, and she was half-
Spanish, exotic. He had come all the way from Edinburgh
especially for this. And why did Amelia love Rae? Because he
spoke about strange things, because of smoking the hubble-bubble
pipe. There was something *Arab* about this young Scottish man.
Something Arab that Amelia had wanted for years. For she had
grown up in the splendid villa of her parents, secretly and guiltily
eyeing the house-boys, fancying the gardener from Fez.

Rae and Amelia provided the international community with the
spiciest piece of gossip of the year. In coffee parties, over tele-

phones, even the men at work spoke of the sudden marriage, the foolish girl. The foolish girl became a sickly wife. Rae pondered morning sickness and could not make sense of it. He held Amelia's hair away from her face as she vomited time and time again into the bathroom sink. Money worried Rae. His brain thought money, money, his heart hurt. He sat up late making calculations, adding and subtracting figures on smudged bits of paper. He got into debt and began to have nightmares about Moroccan prisons. The job at the shop had been adequate for him before, but not now. And what of him, his career. He had vague ideas of becoming a political analyst, a foreign journalist like the ones he met at the shop, travelling the world in search of war and revolution.

Amelia did not take to the presence of the pilots in the flat. 'They *smell*,' she said and sobbed on Rae's shoulders. One evening her mother came and there was a scene, her mother shouting at Rae in Spanish.

In her sickness, Amelia could eat nothing but what her mother cooked. She left the flat days at a time to be looked after in her parents' villa. Rae skulked around in the cafés and in the mosques. His pilot friends assured him he had done the honourable thing. He did not feel honourable, he felt he had messed up his life or that fate had messed up his life. But it was with good nature that he made cocoa for Amelia, tried to make her smile. He was comfortable with domesticity, the feeling of not being alone, sharing the mundane, a bar of soap, the dust that crept into the room.

They did not talk much about the baby. He came into the world with difficulty, a little blue, with no chin, strange-shaped eyes like crescents, a crooked spine. Amelia was not allowed to see him. She never did. Rae never forgot the weightless, mangled bundle, the hair that was thick and dark, the colour of his own hair. He had always thought that babies were born bald, he had not expected so much hair. The hair made him cry in front of Amelia's parents, the doctor and the nurse.

Grief pierced the continuity of his life, for a while burned away even the desire for the World Service. While Amelia recuperated in hospital, he sought, red-eyed, his pilot friends. Their company cooled him. They spoke to him but he could not listen, understand, was content with their voices alone. The things they said. That children who die will intercede for their parents. They will stand at the gates of Paradise and refuse to go in without their mother and father, cry out wanting them, and Allah will grant them their wish.

In the hospital Amelia suffered from the shots they gave her to dry up her milk, from the stitches, from the feeling that all that pain was for nothing. She grieved for the figure she once had, for the happy life of swimming and parties. She blamed Rae, the physically unscathed Rae. Her mother blamed Rae. Everything about him was wrong. Her pretty daughter could have done much better than that. Much, much better. But it was not too late, reasoned the shrewd mother, in fact what had happened to the baby might not be such a bad thing after all. If she acted decisively she could put an end to this silly marriage. She enlisted the help of Rae's employer. The wise scholar pondered and puffed at his pipe. He advised Rae to give up, to leave, to go home and continue with his studies. And Amelia said, 'I don't want you anymore.'

In the years to come, fate for Amelia twisted and held out a Welshman, a bungalow in Gwenyd, daughters and sons. She became an excellent cook like her mother and eventually ran her own catering business. Rae went back to student life, abandoned the plans to become a foreign journalist. Perhaps he had come to discover that under their wordly exterior was a narrowness, a lack of empathy for Morocco. He was too heavy for their globe-trotting world, too deep. It was the ideas and the words that he loved. Marxist, strategic. Guerrilla warfare, resistance. Nationalism. Revolution. *Coup d'état.*

*   *   *

Sammar sat with her head on her knees. She thought of that silent baby, a European buried in African sand. She said on the telephone, 'How can you like a place, visit it again, study its culture and history when something horrible happened to you there?'

He was quiet.

When he spoke, he said, 'Because it was healthy for me, like medicine. It made me less hard. And I learnt things I could not have learnt from books. Like you.'

She did not understand. 'What, about me?' she asked. And again he said, 'You make me feel safe. I feel safe with you.'

7

S ammar walked to work wearing her new coat, conscious of how clean it was, how the wool was not faded or worn out. In the shop windows, she saw her reflection, the coat's henna-red colour, the toggles instead of buttons. She felt like when she was young on the first day of the Eid, new dress, new socks, a new ribbon for her hair. At the pelican crossing when she was waiting for the lights to change, she took off her glove and put her hand in her pocket to feel the fresh silkiness of the lining. Green man, the sound of an alarm clock, and she crossed the road, putting her glove back on. It was too cold for bare fingers, January cold, even though the day was mild for this time of year and she had decided to walk instead of taking the bus as she usually did. A still day with a downcast sky, no sun. She had learnt early on, from the first year she had come with Tarig, that the winter sun of this city was colder than its winter rains. Many times before that lesson was learnt, she had seen the bright sun from the window, felt its warmth through the glass and gone out lightly dressed, only to shiver with incomprehension and suffer as every inadequately dressed African suffers in the alien British cold.

There was still the remains of a holiday atmosphere, the Christmas lights not yet taken down. No schoolchildren, no lollipop ladies, the term had not yet begun. Sammar knew that when she got to the

63

university it would be quiet and dull with the students still away until next week. She would walk the corridors of the buildings meeting only other staff or the odd postgraduate student. The lecture rooms would be dark and silent, the library without its usual liveliness. She would meet Rae and he would not be as busy as he was during term time. She would ask him about his cold, his cough had sounded worse the last time they spoke. He would show her the University of Azhar thesis that he wanted her to start working on, she would give him the book on the Qudsi Hadiths, and there would still be time. Maybe they could talk like they had talked on the telephone, she saying what she had always wanted to say and he not surprised. Listening to her and then talking about places and people she could never have known, making her feel that she could understand them, that she was connected to his stories in some way. Maybe they could talk in his office like they had talked on the telephone. She had not counted the times he had called her over the holidays, nor measured their conversations in minutes and hours. She had stopped herself from doing that. And she had stopped herself from asking, why is he calling me, what is going to happen, what does all this mean?

The shops were beginning to open their doors. Sammar passed a newsagent, a sports shop, fishmonger, bakery. The grocer shop which sold halal meat was closed; it opened late in the day. Sometimes on her way home, she stopped there. While the Bengali owner of the shop cut up the chicken at the back, she would stand waiting near the counter, the small dingy space cramped with sacks of dried vegetables, tins from faraway places, around her the smell of spices and Asian film stars on the walls. She bought chili sauce and tins of beans, the ingredients written out in Arabic, packed in a warm place on another continent. A packet of mix for *falafel*, made in Alexandria.

She walked past a shoe shop, a shop selling wedding dresses and lingerie. Winter bargains, the January Sale, big red signs, half-price, 30 per cent off, Biggest Ever Sale. Yesterday, she had been one of the people in search of bargains. Yesterday had been a busy day. In the morning when she woke, she had looked with clear eyes at her room, the hospital room. She had seen the ugly curtains, the faded bedspread. She opened cupboard and drawers to find tired elastic, worn-out nylon and scruffy shoes with eroded heels. She held these things in her hands, as if seeing them for the first time. Frayed wools, discoloured cottons, and even her scarves, the silks for her hair which she had always chosen with care were now dull and threadbare. Since Tarig died she had not bought anything new. She had not noticed time moving past, the years eroding the clothes Tarig had seen her in, wools he had touched, colours he had given his opinion on.

The kitchenette in the corner of the room held a small fridge, the electric ring, the table she used as a desk. There she saw the mouldy bread, cheese with fur and green, salad that had grown dark and heavy, past its sell-by date. Things did not have a smell in this part of the world. If she had been back home, she would not have been able to be neglectful for so long and the ants and the cockroaches would not have left her in peace. Here, an onion had grown a long green stalk. A chicken leg, three months old, sat in the fridge like rubber. Only the ancient cucumber oozed a puddle of toffee-like substance, but it still did not have a smell. For years, Sammar had eaten such food, hacking away at the good bits and not questioned what she was doing, as if there were a fog blocking her vision, a dreamy heaviness everywhere. Now she looked around the hospital room and said to herself, 'I am not like this. I am better than this.'

Big black bags, putting things away, folding and putting things away in a bag. Like when Tarig died and she had stripped everything away, mistakenly thinking she was never coming back to Aberdeen. But now there was no grief, no burning in her head and chest, she worked calmly, decided what she wanted to keep and what she didn't. It did not take long. It was easy. She then cleaned everything, the floors and the walls, the windows and the fridge, the cupboard, the drawers. She made everything smell of soap and opened the windows to rinse her life with the freezing rain. She pulled the curtain down and took the pillow and the blanket to the launderette.

It was strange to walk into the big department stores, their bright lights and the smell of perfume, crowds of people in search of bargains. She was pleased that the shops were crowded. Quiet shops where the attendants had the time to say 'Can I help you?' made her nervous. When she bought the coat, she had a choice between different styles and colours. One coat which suited her when she tried it on, had golden buttons, their colour and cool touch a reminder of her aunt. In the dressing room with the mirrors behind her and in front of her, too many reflections of herself, she missed her aunt, suddenly and painfully, wished that they were together, that she could hug her again, that they could be close again, friends, like in the years before Tarig died. But Sammar did not buy the coat with the golden buttons though she knew her aunt would have preferred it and her aunt's taste in clothes had always been the ideal, the guidance. She bought the duffle coat with the toggles and the smooth brown stones instead of buttons. After she paid for it and left the shop, she lifted it out of the large plastic bag with the red letters SALE and put it on straightaway, tearing off the price tags, stuffing her old coat in its place.

'You have lovely skin,' said the bright lady behind the cosmetics counter. She had a lot of mascara on very few eyelashes. She tapped the jars and the bottles of lotions with her long fuchsia nails.

'Oh . . . thank you.'

'You won't need these,' the lady continued and her delicate hand hovered over lotions and creams in purple containers. 'This one,' and she picked up a bottle of yellow lotion. 'Try it.'

Sammar tipped the bottle and rubbed a little of the lotion on the back of her hand.

'Do you wear make-up?'

'No . . . I used to . . .'

'Because if you buy the moisturiser, the soap and the toner, you get a gift set with lipstick, blusher, eyeliner and eye shadow. It's a special offer.' The fuchsia nails pointed to a sign that stood on the counter: 'Special Offer' written in red and a picture of the gift set looking bigger than it was in real life.

Sammar had not worn make-up or perfume since Tarig died four years ago. Four months and ten days, was the sharia's mourning period for a widow, the time that was for her alone, time that must pass before she could get married again, beautify herself again. Four months and ten days. Sammar thought, as she often thought, of the four months and ten days, such a specifically laid out time, not too short and not too long. She thought of how Allah's sharia was kinder and more balanced than the rules people set up for themselves.

She bought new curtains for her room. When she hung them up, they changed the room, changed the light in it. It was now no longer a hospital room with the coloured plastic bags and packaging scattered on the floor, her new scarves laid out on the bed. Then, looking at the curtains, their bright pattern of orange, blue and brown, she realised that they were like the curtains Rae had described to her, the curtains that had been in his old house overlooking the Dee. She had unconsciously chosen these colours, the same colours he had talked about. His words were in her mind now, floating, not evaporating away. At night she dreamt no longer of the past but of the rain and grey colours of his city. She dreamt of the present. She dreamt of Lesley saying that the telephone in the hall did not work anymore. She dreamt that she, and not Amelia, was the one who was carrying the dead, disfigured baby. He was heavy inside her and she wanted to push him out. But her aunt was there in the dream saying, you are not due yet, it is still not time to give birth. Her aunt did not know that the baby was dead, only Sammar knew because Rae had told her. She wasn't sad, she felt the baby's heaviness dragging down and the pain was familiar, not frightening, not unpleasant. She knew that her aunt

67

was wrong, that it was time now and she would not be able to stop herself from pushing the baby out.

The dreams were good for her, stinging like antiseptic. She gathered the courage to telephone a driving school, book a first lesson. The instructor, a large, lively woman with white hair, took her to an empty stretch of road near Hazelhead park. It came back to her, the driving she had been taught by 'Am Ahmed, changing gears, the nice sound the hand-brake made when it was pulled. But when they went out onto a busier road, she panicked every time a car passed her in the opposite direction. She would cringe at the sight of the approaching car, turn the steering wheel to the left and instinctively go over the *shahadah: I bear witness there is no god but Allah . . .* while the instructor reached to steady the steering wheel with her hand. When Rae telephoned that evening of her first lesson, she was in tears, 'I've forgotten everything, I'll never learn, I'll never pass any driving test.' He laughed at her and said, 'Of course you'll learn, it will all come back. Don't say you're stupid, you're not stupid.' He said encouraging things while her tears made the receiver slippery in her hand.

Sammar walked to work through familiar streets. She knew where the road changed from asphalt to cobbles. Even certain people's faces had become familiar over time. Years ago, these same streets were a maze of culture shocks. Things that jarred – an earring on a man's earlobe, a woman walking a dog big enough to swallow the infant she was at the same time pushing in a pram, the huge billboards on the roads: Wonderbra, cigarette ads that told people to smoke and not smoke at the same time, the Ministry of Sin nightclub housed in a former church. Now Sammar did not notice these things, did not gaze at them, alarmed, as she had done years before. Her eyes had grown numb over the years and she had found out, gradually, and felt reassured, that she was not alone, that not everyone believed what the billboards said, not everyone understood why that woman kept such a large ferocious dog in her home.

8

T he campus was quiet as she had expected it to be, not so many cars parked in the car park, the department building empty of students. Sammar's room was on the top floor, where a window looked straight up at the sky. She liked her room because of the sunlight that came from that window. She shared the room with Diane, one of Rae's Ph.D. students. To Sammar's surprise, the room was open, the lights were on and Diane was hunched over some photocopied sheets, surrounded by her usual accessories of pens, Diet Coke, Yorkie bars, a ham and pickle sandwich.

'I thought you would be away; it's nice to see you.' Sammar hung her coat up on the hook behind the door. 'What happened? Didn't you go home?' Home for Diane was Leeds.

'I did but I came back last night.' She held her face in her hand, looking up at Sammar.

'You look tired.'

'Too many late nights, too many parties.' Diane smiled, took off her glasses, sniffed and put her head down on the desk. She had straight blonde hair and it fell now and slipped over the pages on the desk. Without her glasses she looked younger and less studious. Sammar was conscious of how young Diane was, nearly eight years her junior and so independent in comparison to how

Sammar had been at that age. Independent and another source of culture shock that had mellowed over time. '. . . I bought my mum knickers for Christmas', '. . . met him at the pub', '. . . hardly *anyone* showed up for Rae's lecture this morning, there was a big piss-up last night', '. . . I definitely don't want to have children. I am *never* going to get married'. Diane repeated that last sentence often, something that she felt strongly about. Had Sammar been back home and Diane one of her old friends, she would have replied, 'Are you mad? You want to live celibate all your life!' and they both would have started laughing. Here, she just said quietly to Diane, 'Maybe you'll change your mind and get married one day.'

'Did you go anywhere?' Diane now asked.

'No,' but Sammar felt that she had been away, far away to a place where she was content. She switched on the computer that was on her desk, pushed the button on the monitor and the screen flickered. The computer began its memory check. 'I am going away early next month. I'm going to Cairo then I'll go to Khartoum and bring my son back with me.' Diane put on her glasses and looked at her with sleepy eyes. She yawned.

'So is it a problem getting your son in, immigration and all that.'

'No, he was born here. So was I.'

'Really? I didn't know.'

'Didn't I ever mention it? My father was studying here at the time. That's how I got a British passport. They've changed the law now. But back then, everyone who was born in Britain was eligible for a passport. So it's no problem about bringing my son.'

Diane looked disappointed as if she had been expecting a hard-luck story about the injustice of the Home Office.

If it had not been for the passport, Sammar would not have been here now. It was because coming back to live in Britain was feasible that she had got on the plane after quarrelling with her aunt, sold her gold bracelets for the one-way ticket. She had chosen

Aberdeen for the tie with Tarig and because she had worked temporarily for the university and there was a chance that they could give her work again. She had been lucky. There was a demand for translating Arabic into English, not much competition. Her fate was etched out by a law that gave her a British passport, a point in time when the demand for people to translate Arabic into English was bigger than the supply. 'No,' she reminded herself, 'that is not the real truth. My fate is etched out by Allah Almighty, if and who I will marry, what I eat, the work I find, my health, the day I will die are as He alone wants them to be.' To think otherwise was to slip down, to feel the world narrowing, dreary and tight.

She scrolled through her files, clicked with the mouse the one that she wanted. Diane was talking about the last time she saw Rae before she went to Leeds.

'. . . not in the best of moods. I wanted to get some papers from him and he said, "You can find them in the library, I haven't got them." But I know he has them. Then all I got from him was a lecture on how the library does not close *every single day* of the holidays.'

Sammar smiled as Diane groaned and put her head down on the desk.

'*And* he gave me this.' She waved in front of Sammar a student essay with a yellow post-it note attached to it. Sammar read Rae's handwriting on the little note, 'Diane, fourteen is far too generous for such a poorly-referenced essay.' Diane took the tutorials for one of Rae's undergraduate classes and sometimes she had to mark the students' work.

'How much does he want you to give it then?' said Sammar.

'Eleven at the most.' Diane starting taking out her sandwich from its packaging.

'Well, eleven is a pass, isn't it?'

'I want to encourage her. Fourteen would have encouraged her but the bastard is just so finicky.'

'Maybe she could rewrite it.'

'She won't do that, she'll just take the eleven.' Diane dropped the essay back on the far corner of her desk and eating her sandwich, bent her head down over her work.

Sammar was glad that Diane was back. She did not like being alone and it always pleased her when Diane mentioned Rae. It was like when Yasmin talked about him only that Diane was spontaneous and not suspicious, while Yasmin had recently begun to frown disapprovingly every time Sammar asked her about Rae, snapping, 'Are you expecting him to become a Muslim so he could marry you?' Sammar wondered if Yasmin was back from Manchester, where she had gone with Nazim to visit his parents. Later, on her way home, she would go to Rae, see if he was back, pass the secretaries' office and see if Yasmin was also back.

In the afternoon she went to pray in the small university mosque, a room given over to the Muslim students. It was in another building, older and more beautiful than the modern building where her own department was. She found the room dark and empty. She switched on the lights, took off her shoes and felt eerily alone in the spacious room with its high ceiling. When it was crowded during term time, everyone just prayed on the carpet, but now she took one of the mats that were folded on a shelf and spread it out. It was blue, plusher than the one she had at home and with a picture of the Ka'ba under a navy sky. There was more reward praying in a group than praying alone. When she prayed with others, she found it easier to concentrate, her heart held steady by those who had faith like her. Now she stood alone under the high ceiling of the ancient college, began to say silently, *All praise belongs to Allah, Lord of all the worlds, the Compassionate, the Merciful* . . . and the certainty of the words brought unexpected tears, something deeper than happiness, all the splinters inside her coming together.

When she finished praying, she looked at the notices on the notice board: the prayer timetable, the dates of meetings of the inter-faith group, a talk on Jerusalem with a speaker coming up from St Andrews.

She walked back to her room through the wet gardens of the campus. Being outdoors in the fresh air was a break in the day, it was colder than it had been in the morning. On days when Diane was not in, Sammar prayed in the room, locking the door from inside. She had an old shawl which she kept in the drawer of her desk and used as a prayer mat. It had seemed strange for her when she first came to live here, all that privacy that surrounded praying. She was used to seeing people pray on pavements and on grass. She was used to praying in the middle of parties, in places where others chatted, slept or read. But she was aware now, after having lived in this city for many years she could understand, how surprised people would be were they to turn the corner of a building and find someone with their forehead, nose and palms touching the ground. She wondered how Rae would feel if he ever saw her praying. Would he feel alienated from her, the difference between them accentuated, underlined, or would it seem to him something that was within reach, something that he himself would want to do?

She switched the computer off and the room lost the steady humming sound that had filled it all day. Diane was at the library and the room without the computer was silent. Sammar was ready to go home and to pass by Rae's office on the way but she continued sitting. Perhaps he would be different than he had been on the telephone, cooler, more formal, distracted by other things. Maybe the way he talked to her on the telephone was to do with the holidays. These dark mid-winter holidays when everything was closed, and the days were the shortest in the whole year. Days that fell away from normality, gave way to excess.

Diane pushed open the door and came in carrying two bars of Yorkie and a packet of crisps.

'I just met Yasmin at the ref,' she dropped her snacks on the desk.

'She's back then.'

'She's looking real big now,' Diane sat down and turned in her swivel chair.

'Really?' smiled Sammar and then, 'No, thank you' to Diane's offer of a Yorkie bar.

'She said that Rae's in hospital.'

The pain came into a specific place, the top of her stomach. 'Why?'

Diane pulled open her packet of crisps. The smell of cheese and onions filled the room. 'Apparently some nurse phoned from Foresterhill and said that he had this real bad asthma attack and they're keeping him in because he's also got bronchitis. So,' went on Diane, 'that sounds like a fine start to his New Year. I don't know who's going to take over his classes next week if he's not back by then. Yasmin kind of thought that they wouldn't keep him long.'

Sammar stared at the carpet, an indentation where the chair's leg had stood. He had been coughing on the telephone, coughing and saying that he was feverish and she had not guessed that it was serious. If Diane had not said 'that's a fine start to his New Year', had not filled the room with the smell of cheese and onions, perhaps then it would not hurt so much or there would not be anger mixed with the hurt. She wanted to say, 'You have no manners, you are rude. When someone is taken ill, when there is bad news, there are certain things that must be said, a sympathetic word, a good wish for them. When that person is someone older than you, your professor, someone who helps you, then you should be doubly respectful. Not so callous, you are not a child to be so callous.' She pressed her teeth together. 'Don't speak,' she told herself, 'you are not allowed to speak like that.' She felt the blood gushing to her nose as if she was about to have a nose-bleed. She wanted it, the soft pluck noise, the sticky blood released from her nose.

'I'll go now,' she said and put her coat on, picked up her bag. 'Bye.'

'See you.'

When she closed the door behind her, liquid dribbled from her nose, but it was clear as tears. Down the stairs, in the street, on the bus, she told herself that she was overreacting, that there was no need for this. He would be all right in a week or two. Bronchitis was not such a terrible thing. She shivered in the lit streets, in the bus that was too slow. The bus stopped too long at traffic lights, it patiently let people climb in and out. Ordinary life, an ordinary day. The passengers seemed to her to be superhuman, people walking around not lumbered with pain. She did not want to cry on the bus in front of them.

She pushed the key into the lock of the building. Loud music, heavy metal. Some of the tenants were back, the Christmas break over. A letter from her aunt, colourful African stamps damp with Europe's rain. The post, sluggish during the holidays was now regular again. She put the letter unopened in her handbag, walked up the stairs. Her room was no longer a hospital room it had new curtains, a new bedspread. She must not cry. What was there to cry about? Talk to herself, 'Don't be silly.' The music came down through the ceiling. Grating, angry. Why were they angry? She couldn't understand. She must get away from the music. She knew where she was going to go. Talk to herself, 'Stop crying, what is there to cry about? Your eyes will be red. He will see you and your eyes will be ugly and red.'

9

Foresterhill was a large complex of hospital buildings. It was interspersed by roads, cars and buses, car parks, bus stops, gardens and a children's playground. There was the Medical School where Tarig had trained and sat exams, there was the Maternity Hospital where Sammar had Amir. There was Casualty where Tarig had died on a sunny day and she had sat waiting for someone to come from the mosque, while Amir roamed the corridors, touching everything, playing with the fire extinguisher, until she picked him up, shook him and hissed, 'I wish it was you instead, you are so easily replaceable.' But he had wriggled away from her, too young to understand, too good-natured to be disturbed by her anger. Only she was left with guilt, dirty like metal.

Sammar pushed her way to the hospital. It felt like that, even though she sat in the warm bus, not walking, not running, not exerting herself. She must not think of the last time she had come here. It had been different, it was daylight then, summer, and she had come wearing sandals, pushing Amir in his pushchair. Now she was coming by bus, alone, and it was winter darkness outside the bus, freezing cold. Why was she going to see Rae? If he was asleep would she just sit on a chair, listen to him snore? If he was very ill, would he not be irritated by her presence, that she was seeing him like that, intruding on something private? What if he looked at her in a surprised way, his eyes asking, what are you doing here?

She should go back home. She should get off the bus at the next bus stop, cross the road and catch another bus going in the opposite direction. To encourage herself, she used cunning, ruses. 'You can go to him another day,' she told herself, 'when he is more recovered. Maybe Yasmin could come with you or even Diane (somehow she doubted that), the other students then, the Algerian lady, then it would look more respectable, people from work coming to see him. It would seem natural then.' She said to herself, 'There is nothing wrong with admitting that you have acted rashly in coming out like this to see him. It is actually wiser to admit a mistake and retract, than to stubbornly go on. So at the next bus stop get out, stand up now and walk to the door so that when the door opens you can get out straightaway.' But bus stop after bus stop came and went, and she continued sitting, pushing her way to Foresterhill.

The bus stopped in front of the hospital, the automatic doors swished open. She was so slow getting up from her seat, that the doors started to close as she passed through them. They hit her on her shoulder, swung back open again and the bus driver scowled at her through his rear mirror, muttered under his breath.

A glass door to push in order to get inside the building. The heaviest glass door in the world. Her shoulder felt bruised. There was a gift shop in the foyer: stuffed toys, flowers, a shop which sold newspapers and sweets. Lifts to the different wards. She suddenly realised that she did not know which ward Rae was in. This realisation came as a relief. If she could not find him then it would be a sign that she should not have come and she would go away, convinced. If she found his ward, she would ask if he was well enough for visitors, if not, she would go away without leaving her name. If he was asleep she would go away before he woke up. She felt better now. She had sorted everything out.

'I want to visit someone but I don't know which ward they are in,' she said to the nurse at the reception. The nurse asked her questions, a man or a woman, what did he have, when was he admitted, his name. She checked what looked like computer print-outs and gave Sammar a ward number.

'Is he well enough for visitors?' Wide eyes.

'You will have to ask at the ward itself. They'll tell you.' An impatient smile.

Many people were waiting for the lifts. Near the lifts was a Christmas tree and a café busy with people drinking and eating. Others sat on settees, chatting and reading newspapers. The bustle reminded Sammar of airports. It was hard to believe that people suffered within these walls.

At the ward, she gave his name to the nurse. The nurse had a young pretty face, clear blue eyes. She was so thin that her stomach, held in by the wide red belt of her uniform, looked concave.

'There he is, fifth bed on the right.' The nurse pointed her finger down the ward but Sammar did not look to where she was pointing.

'Is he well enough for visitors?'

'Oh yes, he's fine.' Surprise in the eyes of the nurse.

The nurse hovered a little and Sammar had to start walking away from that look of surprise. Head down, eyes down, grey linoleum, count the beds by counting their legs. One, two, three. She looked up and her eyes took in the whole ward. Straight in front of her, a Christmas tree near a large window. A row of beds either side of a long aisle. Some of the beds had green curtains around them, their occupants hidden away. The rest was a sea of ill men on beds with white sheets, their faces blurred together, indistinguishable. She saw him before he saw her. He was sitting up, not connected to machines or drips. He looked so strikingly familiar that she caught her breath. Here he was, someone that she knew from somewhere else. She knew him better than anyone else here did. She knew him separately from this place. Here he was, someone that was connected to her. So that the first words she said to him did not belong to the rational world. 'Rae, why did they bring you here?' He said her name, then his voice got louder, 'I am so pleased to see you, it's great to see you.' He kept repeating himself and his voice was so loud that she became embarrassed imagining that the ward was shifting, its people turning and looking at them. She wanted to bend down and put her arms around him, say to him, lower your voice, you're speaking too loudly. Instead she put her hands in her pockets and sat on the chair that was next to his bed.

He looked older than she remembered, or maybe she was noticing only now that there was white in his hair. Greasy today, longer than usual, shine on the skin of his forehead and nose. He was wearing grey pyjamas, crumpled and with one of the buttons missing, a black T-shirt underneath. He smiled at her, his lips almost blue and there was a darkness too on his cheeks, the tips of his fingers. He looked happy to see her.

She said, 'Your voice is very loud,' and looked anxiously across at his neighbour. He was an elderly man asleep on his side facing them. He looked like he wore false teeth when he wasn't sleeping. On the other side of Rae, was a bed with a green curtain wrapped around it, across the aisle a young man was reading a newspaper.

Rae did not answer, only smiled and kept looking at her. She looked away. Welcoming her had made him wheezy. He coughed, one small cough, but it was a horrible sound, worse than any time she had heard him cough before.

'What happened, tell me.'

He shook his head and said, short of breath, 'In a while . . . you talk.'

She did not know what to say, what to start talking about. If he would not look at her, it would be easy to talk.

'Do you want to know how I found out that you were in hospital?'

'Yes.'

She told him, at the same time twisting the strap of her handbag, which was on her lap as if she was ready to get up and leave at any minute. Her handbag reminded her of her aunt's letter and she became conscious of it, lying unopened inside her bag.

'You look nice,' he said.

This was sudden and made her feel shy. She said, 'It's my new coat, I got it half price at the Sale.'

He laughed, his laugh trailed off into another cough. He pressed his thumb against his chest, grimaced and said, 'This hurts.'

She thought, 'I must not say anything that could make him laugh. Laughing makes him cough.' They were quiet, neither of them speaking. Time passed. She felt like she had travelled miles to get here, struggled, pushed her way through fog and quicksand. Now that she had arrived, she felt settled, her heart and mind settled, no swishing thoughts. Everything was here now, filling up the silent time. Minute after minute and the smell of disinfectant. Hospital sounds: footsteps, trolleys, people's voices, the ringing of a telephone far away. A telephone that had nothing to do with them. She stopped twisting the strap of her handbag. She smiled at him and looked away. It was not a dream, her eyes and ears were calm, missing nothing.

'What is that on your hand?' she asked. He had a plaster on the back of his left hand.

'I've been getting amoxyillin through an intravenous drip, but from tomorrow I'll be getting it as pills to swallow.' He seemed more able to talk now and he told her how his chest had got worse in the last few days, how the drive from Stirling to Aberdeen had been a nightmare ending in the biggest asthma attack he had ever had.

'I drove straight to the GP and he referred me here. I haven't even gone home yet. I still have all my things with me.'

'You should have seen a doctor in Stirling; you shouldn't have driven back if you were feeling so ill.'

He didn't answer her and instead said, 'I just remembered I have something for you, right here with me now.'

He got up from the bed slowly. She saw that he was wearing socks, odd colours, one navy and one black. He bent down and pulled a suitcase from underneath the bed. He opened it and started to pull out from it clothes, what looked like his laundry, a jumble of books and tapes.

'I am usually more organised than this,' he said.

Sammar had to bite her lips to stop herself from offering to take his laundry home, wash his clothes for him. She wanted to fold them, smooth them out, align the sleeves together, sort them into piles.

'Can I look at your tapes? Is this what you listen to in the car?'

He nodded and went on searching his suitcase. She recognised some of his tapes, Bob Marley's *Survival, Babylon By Bus, Uprising.* He drove around Scotland listening to reggae; the call for Africa to unite . . . ambush in the night . . . we'll be forever loving Jah. The words came back to her with their tunes . . . *Emancipate yourselves from mental slavery, none but ourselves can free our minds* . . . Where had she heard these songs? Back home, in the petrol queues of Souk 2, from the radio of a Toyota pickup, the cars bumper to bumper, the whole queue like a segmented snake burning under the sun. The smell from the bakery mixed with the smell of oil, and petrol fume addicts squatting near the fuming pumps, beggars leaning on the cars, thrusting their fingers through the windows. There were the songs and here in this cold city Tarig bought the tapes from a shop on Union Street, for the ones back home had long ago melted in the sun. Look out at the dark rain, hope that

Tarig was doing well in his exam and teach Amir to sing, *Sun is shining, the weather is sweet* . . .

She held one of the tapes in her hand, opened and closed the box. Flags of Africa on the cover, green, so many of them green. Reds, blue, crescents and stars, a torch held up high. In her own hospital room, on good days, she had played that same tape, someone telling the truth, *by the power of the Most High we keep on surfacing.*

'I got you this from Edinburgh,' said Rae.

It was wrapped in light-blue paper, square shaped, a little box. He began to put his things back into the bag, slowly but carelessly stuffing them away.

She unwrapped the present, careful not to tear the paper. It was a bottle of perfume, oval shaped, with a stopper not an atomiser, liquid the colour of amber. She had thought all the time he was looking in his bag that he was going to give her the Azhar thesis he wanted her to translate. She said, 'Thank you,' and opened the bottle. The scent was neither fresh nor spicy but heavy and sweet. 'It smells nice,' she told him, even though she knew that this was not the way to judge perfume, she should first rub it on the inside of her wrist, wait for it to settle. But she could not do that now and looking up she saw that he was as embarrassed as she was.

He said, still kneeling on the ground putting his bag away, 'The man who sold it to me was French. He said, this perfume is new, it's the best, it's come from Heaven via Paris.'

She laughed, 'What a funny thing to say, from Heaven via Paris.'

He looked tired when he stood up, sat down again on the bed. She said, 'I should go now, you look tired.'

He shook his head. 'No please stay. It's just that standing up suddenly made me dizzy. Stay, I want to talk to you.'

She folded the gift paper and put it away with the perfume inside her handbag. She took out her aunt's letter. 'Look what my aunt wrote as the address. "Aberdeen, England" and someone at the postoffice went over England in red ink.'

'You have just won me to your side, Sammar, in any quarrel you've had with your aunt. Aberdeen, England, is unforgivable.'

'That's what they must have thought at the post office. It's a good thing they delivered it.'

'When I was in Cairo,' he said, 'I was often asked, are you English, *Ingelizi?* and I would say, No. *Amrikani?* No. Then they would start getting suspicious. I'd say Scottish and they'd say, Oh, is that where the war is?'

'*Scotlandi,*' she said. 'You should say, *Ana Scotlandi mish Irelandi.*'

'Tell me before I forget,' he said, 'what does *shirk al-asbab* mean? I know that *shirk* means polytheism.'

' *Asbab* are causes, intermediaries, so *shirk al-asbab* means the polytheism of intermediaries. For example to believe in Nature, to elevate Nature which is only an intermediary and set it up as a kind of partner to God. Where did you come across it?'

'Fareed.'

'Is he the one you met in Stirling?'

'Yes. He's going to be coming to Aberdeen later this month to teach part of my course. You'll meet him then. I spoke to him about you.'

She wondered why he had spoken about her, how he put her into words.

'Where is he from, originally?'

'He came here from Lebanon. But he is originally a Palestinian from Gaza. He was a journalist and he was imprisoned by the Israelis for some time. They gave him a rough time, a real rough time.'

She said, 'Have you been to Gaza or Lebanon?'

'No.'

'My aunt went to Beirut long ago, before all the troubles. She bought me so many things.' Her aunt had brought her a T-shirt with a round yellow smiling face, a doll that could walk. ' I forgot I haven't even opened her letter.'

She wanted to read the letter now so that his presence could cushion the inevitable hurt.

The letter was brief, with an attached list of things that her aunt wanted her to bring. Items from the pharmacy: paracetamol, laxatives, biscuits for diabetes. Also Hanan had just had a baby and seemed to need the whole of Mothercare. Then there were things for Amir: clothes, roller blades. Roller blades? How did they find out about things like that? Sammar put the list of orders back into the envelope, it was too daunting. Her aunt must imagine that she was making millions, an expatriate like those who found jobs in Saudi Arabia and the Gulf. The letter itself was breezy, 'I am so proud that you got this job to go to Egypt, wonderful that they are going to pay for your ticket! This is the right thing, as I've said before, to concentrate on your career and your son. It will be good for him to be in England with you, good for his education. So many envy you.' This was followed by a torrent of complaints about life in Khartoum and how awful Sammar would find it after being away for so long. Then the last lines: 'I am so glad you seem to have got rid of this ridiculous idea of getting married again – when you see Amir, how lovable he is, you will not have the hard heart to be so selfish and bring him a stepfather, some stranger who will not treat him well. Of course it doesn't matter where you are, no one is seeing you there but when you come, it would be better not to wear so much colour, you know how people get ideas. You don't need to get everything that Hanan has asked for, she wants too much as usual, but my pharmacy things be sure to bring them.'

Sammar smiled weakly at Rae. She wanted to speak but couldn't.

'So what is the news?' he said.

'My aunt thinks that Amir would like roller blades.'

He said that Mhairi had roller blades and went on to talk about children's toys. She listened to his voice but not what he was saying.

'My aunt thinks that after living here for so long, I will hate it when I go back to Khartoum. She thinks I will see everything as ugly and backward.'

'I don't think you will see everything as ugly and backward. What do you think?'

'I don't know.'

'Your aunt doesn't know you,' he said.

'She's known me for most of my life!' She pretended that she did not agree with him while inside her she was thrilled by what he had said. She had wanted him to cushion the hurt from the letter and he had done more than that, effortlessly, easily, as if by magic.

'What were you going to tell me before?' she said.

'When?'

'When you told me to stay?'

'Yes, I was going to tell you about Fareed. I started to but I didn't go on. I've known him for years now, we've written some papers together. Every once in a while, he would suddenly have this outburst. Why haven't I accepted Islam, how can I study it, know it and still not see that it is the truth, and wasn't I afraid when the time comes, when I die and I will be asked, wasn't I afraid that I would not have an excuse, I would not be able to plead ignorance? Anyway, he goes through all this with me every once in a while.'

Sammar winced at hearing her own thoughts crudely put by someone else. She looked at Rae, questioningly, wary, why was he telling her all this?

'Well, I was just wondering,' he looked away, 'I was wondering why you don't say things like that?'

She struggled to find an answer. She could say so many things. Things that would be truthful and yet not truthful at the same time. She said, 'Yasmin once told me that it annoys you when

Muslims expect you to convert just because you know so much about Islam.'

'And you are afraid of annoying me?'

'Yes.'

He said, 'The arrogance annoys me,' then he was silent like someone who had more to say but was choosing not to speak.

'Is Fareed very arrogant then?'

'No. No, I would not describe him as arrogant. The reason he goes on is that I view the Qur'an as a sacred text, as the word of God. It would be impossible in the kind of work I'm doing, in the issues I'm addressing for me to do otherwise but accept Muslims' own vision of the Qur'an, what they say about it. To Fareed, though, this is tantamount to accepting Islam, and so he can't understand it when I say I am not a Muslim.'

Sammar couldn't understand it either. Hesitantly she said, 'I think I agree with your friend.'

'Why?'

She wanted to say, because unless you become a Muslim we will not be able to get married, we will not be together and I will be miserable and alone. But she said. 'It would be good for you, it will make you stronger.'

He was quiet and she thought, 'I have hurt him now. I have said the wrong thing.'

A visitor arrived for the elderly man in the next bed, his wife. She nodded at Rae, straightened the blanket that covered her sleeping husband, sat down and after taking out her glasses from her bag started reading a book. Someone had switched on the television that was perched up on the wall at the far end of the ward. Horse-racing, the sound of galloping hoofs, the voice of the commentator.

'Some of these horses have Arab names,' Rae said.

They spoke about the names of horses, Sammar watching his face, making sure that she had not hurt him by what she had said.

She had been given the chance to say something intelligent about Islam and she had lost it. She could have said things about truth, or eternal relevance or about distinguishing faith from cultural traditions. Instead, she had said something personal, 'it will make you stronger', words that carried criticism. She despised herself.

'I have to go now. It looks like you are going to have dinner.' The young nurse was pushing a trolley down the aisle, handing out trays. The ward was filling up with the smell of cooked vegetables. Sammar stood up. 'I'm sorry I made you tired, I stayed too long . . .'

'No,' he said, 'you of all people could never make me tired.'

She smiled but she was still a little anxious, 'I can say the wrong things.'

'Don't worry. Don't worry about that . . .'

In a rush she said, 'I feel so bad that when we were speaking on the telephone, I didn't guess that you were so ill. I thought it was just flu. I should have known.'

'But I myself didn't know. I thought it was just a chest infection. I get them frequently. I must admit I got a scare this time. Breathing in and the air just wouldn't get through. I thought that's it, my card's been called.'

'You were wrong.' She forgot that a few minutes ago she had despised herself.

Downstairs, in the hospital foyer there were mirrors along one wall. Her eyes were a little pink, but their lids were as if rimmed by kohl and there was colour on her lips and cheekbones as if she was wearing make-up. She carried in her handbag a small bottle, sold by a man in Edinburgh who told his customers that the perfume had come all the way from Heaven, via Paris.

'What's this about you visiting Rae in hospital?' Yasmin sat on the only armchair in the room watching Sammar ironing.

'How did you know?'

'Who doesn't know! He's been telling everyone.'

He was back at work now, but only coming in for the lectures. 'Then I go home and collapse into bed,' he had told Sammar.

She said to Yasmin, 'Did he tell you himself, what did he say?'

'He said you were very courageous.'

'Me, courageous!' She smiled and sprayed water on the skirt she was ironing. Courageous.

Yesterday, while with him, the department's secretaries had surrounded her, gushed, 'How *sweet* of you, Sammar, to go and visit him,' and she, overwhelmed, had stepped back closer to him, away from their smell of talcum powder and Gold Blend. He looked pleased with himself. When they turned away, he whispered to Sammar, *'Coup d'état.'*

'So speak, what is going on?' Yasmin said.

'You know that *masha' Allah* you look bigger than five months, are you sure you counted right?' Yasmin sitting, looked like something large and round had fallen from the sky on to her lap.

She ignored her and went on 'You are the last person in the world I expected this from. What do you imagine you're doing?'

'Nothing.'

'Are you going to marry someone who's not a Muslim?'

'Of course not, that would be against the sharia.'

'So what's the point then of running off to see him in hospital?'

Sammar managed a smile at the running off to see him, 'I'm being optimistic.'

'Did he tell you he was going to convert?'

'No,' she said lightly. He had not even told her that he wanted to marry her. 'I think he could, why not?'

'Why not? Because someone like him is probably an agnostic if not an atheist. The whole of the department are atheists. These people are so left wing, "religion is the opium of the people" and all that.'

Sammar did not know what agnostic meant. She concentrated on the pleats of the skirt, manoeuvring the iron. She wished Yasmin would talk about something else. And he was to blame for this. She couldn't understand why he was telling everyone that she had been to see him at hospital. At times he seemed to her reserved and secretive, at other times open like this.

Now she would have liked to ask Yasmin about his ex-wife, what colour were her eyes? Instead Yasmin was intent on giving her a lecture of some sort.

'I've seen the kind of Scottish men who marry Muslim girls.' Yasmin went on, 'The typical scenario: he's with an oil company sent to Malaysia or Singapore; she's this cute little thing in a mini-skirt who's out with him every night. Come marriage time, it's by the way I'm a Muslim and my parents will not let you marry me until you convert. And how do I convert, my darling, I love you, I can't live without you? Oh, it's just a few words you have to say. Just say the *shahadah*, it's just a few words: *I bear witness there is no god but Allah and Muhammad is the Messenger of Allah*. End of story.

They get married, and she might as the years go by pray and fast or she might not, but it has nothing to do with him. Everything in his life is just the same as it was before.'

Sammar shrugged, 'It's not the same situation.'

'Is he going to say the *shahadah* without meaning it, just to marry you?'

'I don't know.'

Yasmin didn't say anything in response. She moved her chair to face the bed and put her feet up. Her stockings were a colour Sammar would not wear. Sammar thought that if she had offered to do Rae's laundry for him, his socks would be drying now on the radiators. What would Yasmin have said about that?

'You're leaving in a few weeks' time,' said Yasmin. 'If I were you, I'd avoid him like the plague till then. Go home and maybe you'll meet someone normal, someone Sudanese like yourself. Mixed couples just don't look right, they irritate everyone.'

'But he's very nice. Don't you think he's nice?'

'All that coughing and spluttering gets on my nerves.'

Sammar laughed. 'You're horrible,' she said.

'I'm worried, that's all,' said Yasmin. 'Have you talked to him about becoming a Muslim.'

'Not really, no. But he always says good things about Islam, things I didn't even know. He understands . . .'

'That's his work, the field in which he is very highly thought of. But his interest, as far as I know, is just an academic interest.'

'But it could become more than that . . .'

'Do you know if he even believes in God?'

'Of course he believes in God. He's not empty inside.'

'Atheists can be as nice as anyone else. Being good or kind has nothing to do with it.'

'Also, he told me that he believes that the Qur'an is a sacred text . . .'

'That's the way they do research nowadays. It's a modern thing.

Something to do with not being Eurocentric. They take what each culture says about itself. So they could study all sorts of sacred texts and be detached. They could have their own religious views or be atheists . . .'

'You think Rae is an atheist?'

'I wouldn't be surprised. I would not be surprised at all.'

Sammar put the iron down. Never in her life had anyone she cared about been an unbeliever. Not religious, yes, not praying, not particularly caring about what's right or wrong, but always the faith was there, always Allah was there, His existence never denied. It was unbearable to think that Rae was so unaware.

She left the ironing, hurried and put her coat on, covered her hair with a scarf, rummaged for change from her purse.

'Where are you going?'

His number, where did she have his number? Drawer opened, papers thrown out. She had never telephoned him at home before.

'What's wrong with you, where are you going?'

She found the number, ignored Yasmin. She ran down the stairs to the landing. One of the tenants was getting his bicycle from under the stairs. Leather jacket, long hair tied up with an elastic band, the source of the loud music that came through the ceiling. She was frightened of that man and usually listened and checked that he was not coming up or down the stairs before she left her flat. Now when she saw him she dropped one of her coins on the ground and had to bend down and pick it up. When she stood up, he was sneering at her. Then he jerked his bicycle from under the stairs and rattled away. There were chains around his trousers, the sharp step of his boots. When he opened the front door, a gust of cold wind blew in. She shivered. The telephone. Dialing, her fingers awkward, clumsy. Ringing. It rang and rang. She let it ring. It rang and rang. She shivered and the telephone rang, each unanswered ring cutting through an emptiness, a windy place. At last, a sleepy voice, recognition.

'Rae, do you believe in God?'

In his silence, she banged her head against the wall, gently, rhythmically. The wall felt cool against her forehead, pleasantly solid. The receiver in her hand kept slipping. She thought, I love his voice, he must have been deeply asleep, he is still not well. His voice and how heavy he is inside, heavy enough for me to sink in. All this will be forbidden to me? Where will I . . . She closed her eyes, banged her forehead against the wall. Mid-January and the afternoon light seeped into the hall, the day beginning to get longer, a subtle change in the sun's light. When he spoke, it was as if she had expected the silence to last forever, his clear voice startled her, 'Yes,' he said, 'I do.'

'You're not a . . . an . . . atheist?' She struggled with the word, so seldom used. She mispronounced it.

'No, I'm not.' There was a smile in his voice.

She sat down on the stairs.

'I thought you knew,' he said.

'I wasn't sure.'

'I should have been more clear.'

The landing, the bicycles under the stairs, Yasmin upstairs were superseded. 'I woke you up,' she said. 'You were fast asleep.'

'I dreamt of you.'

'Tell me.'

He said, 'I was in a big house with many rooms. It was almost like a mansion. I was hiding because outside the house, I had been followed, chased for days. I carried a sword in my hand and there was blood on it, my enemies' blood, but I myself, my clothes and my hands were clean and I was proud of that.'

He paused and then went on, 'I went into a room full of smoke, a lot of smoke but when I checked there was no fire. When I left the room, the handle of my sword broke. I held it broken in my hands and knew that it could never be mended, it could never be reliable again. This was a terrible loss, I don't know why, but I had this feeling of deep loss because I had to go on without the sword. I walked the other rooms of the house, searching. There were many rooms, halls, passageways. I found a staircase and I began to climb. At the top of the stairs there was a room and you were there.'

'What was I doing?'

'Cooking.'

She smiled, 'Cooking what?'

'Vegetables, I think.'

She saw green peppers and aubergines. She spoke each word slowly, 'And was I happy to see you?'

'You were, very much and then you gave me a glass of milk to drink.'

'Milk! How childish of me, I'm so sorry.'

He laughed and said, 'I drank it, I drank it all. I didn't mind.'

II

S he made soup for him. She cut up courgettes, celery and onions. Her feelings were in the soup. The froth that rose to the surface of the water when she boiled the chicken, the softened, shapeless tomatoes. Pasta shaped into the smallest stars. Spice that she had to search for, the name unknown in English, not in any of the Arabic–English dictionaries that she had. *Habbahan, habbahan.* She must walk around the supermarket, frantically searching for something she could not ask about, and she was a translator, she should know. *Habbahan.* Without it, the soup would not taste right, would not be complete. At last, she found the *habbahan.* It existed, it had a name: whole green cardamom.

Cardamom pods. They must be split open, the seeds inside crushed into powder. It seemed unfair to her that he was all alone, ill alone, that he dragged himself to teach everyday and came back home to an unmade bed, unwashed cups and dishes, meals that he had to cook himself. In the department they said that he was turning into a workaholic. She said to him, they told you at the hospital to take time off work, why don't you listen? He said that there were too many things that needed to be done.

She put the soup in two plastic containers, carried them to work. She was waiting for him when he came out of the lecture theatre, coughing, his fingers covered in chalk. She saw the change in him, the way he turned his back on everything else, his students who were coming out, the next class that was going in. When he spoke to her it was as if there was no one around, no physical world, his voice different, she had come to realise, than when he talked to others, kind, less sharp. It took him a few minutes to understand what she was saying, what she was carrying, what she was giving to him. Then he said, 'Oh Sammar,' in a low voice, too much emotion. So that they were both, after that, unable to say ordinary things, the usual things, 'thank you very much,' 'I hope you like it,' 'I will like it for sure', 'you can freeze it . . .' She turned and made her way down corridors illuminated with fluorescent lights, crowded with students taller than her, their loose denims, rucksacks, soft hair that fell over young eyes.

Two weeks. Two weeks and she would be far away on another continent. Sunshine, no need to put on the lights indoors. In two weeks' time she would leave this city. She had booked her plane tickets from London, she must book her train ticket from Aberdeen. She had bought the things her aunt had asked for, she must start packing. She thought of going home, seeing home again, its colours again and in spite of years of yearning, all she had now was reluctance and some fear.

12

The past intruded when she wanted only the present. Wanted these two weeks before she left the city. The past came and lined up before her, demanding recognition. The time before she started working in Rae's department. She worked in Languages and sometimes translated things for the Council: English to Arabic, leaflets about the health services, about classes in English. An incident from that time: a Libyan woman in hospital and Sammar was asked to go to Foresterhill and interpret for her. The woman didn't know English and her husband who did was away off-shore. But Sammar refused to go, she could not face the hospital after Tarig. And she drowned her guilt about the Libyan woman in oceans of sleep. In her dreams she forgot that Tarig had died.

Her head in the Languages department was a woman named Jennifer, who one day, unexpectedly and abruptly, called Sammar, asked her to sit down and said that she was not religious but respected people who were religious. That was during the Gulf War, when suddenly everyone became aware that Sammar was Muslim. Once a man shouted at her in King Street, *Saddam Hussein, Saddam Hussein.*

Jennifer said, 'My boyfriend is Nigerian,' and paused as if that statement had a deeper meaning she wanted Sammar to grasp.

Sammar sat and nodded politely. She felt like a child who had stayed up too late at night and was discovering that in the adult world there were things she could not understand. Jennifer talked away fresh and brisk, reassuring her of how broad-minded and tolerant she was, not like so many people. 'For example,' Jennifer said, 'I have no problem at all with the way you dress.'

When Sammar finally spoke, she managed, 'Thank you,' and went home and slept. She slept deeply and continuously until the next day.

It was part of her remit to work for other departments if they needed her. This was how she met Rae when he sent her articles from Arab newspapers, the aftermath of the Gulf War. The first time she went to see him, he surprised her by being not rushed for time, not distracted by other things. She was used to busy people, a tightness in time. Instead, after discussing the newspaper articles, he told her about the time he lived in North Africa and asked her about her name, an unusual name. Lulled by his manner, she said, 'There is a Lebanese ladies' magazine called *Sammar*,' and immediately thought, what a silly thing to say, what an inappropriate thing to say. But he didn't look surprised or amused. He said quite seriously, 'I have not come across this magazine.'

People spoke about him: his students, his secretary, Yasmin. It was through him that Sammar met Yasmin. Yasmin who talked so fluently and knowingly about the Gulf War, immigration, 'these people'. She told Sammar that Rae had been on television several times and on the radio during the war. She would come to work the following morning and the department's answering machine would be jammed with messages, angry voices . . . *You are a disgrace to our universities, we pay taxes . . . You don't know what you're talking about, fighter-planes aren't enough for this war. We need to drop an atomic bomb once and for all . . .* And after a radio programme, Is This War A Holy War?, *You wog bastard, may I remind you that England is a Christian country, and it would be a good thing if you and all the rest of the odious wog bastards were to go back to the land of Allah . Since you bastards came to England this country has become the asshole of the West . . .*

Sammar remembered Yasmin telling her all this in the car one Saturday on the way to a DIY shop, Yasmin mimicking the man's London accent.

'Did Rae get upset?' Sammar had asked.

'No, he laughed.'

And Sammar pictured the scene in the secretaries' office, Yasmin replaying the tape first thing in the morning, Rae standing still wearing his jacket because he had just come in. Some of the blinds in the room would still be drawn, the department still sluggish, no footsteps of students, a few members of staff coming in to check their mail, mumbling greetings, lingering at the sound of the tape. Rae would have listened to the unclear voice on the tape, the message left for him, then laughed alone, for no one else would laugh, and wiped his face with his hand.

Thirteen days to go.

Her date of departure loomed ahead, solid as rock, impressive as a mountain. The days were numbered. They dwindled and by their nature could not increase. But they were not normal days, they expanded as if by magic, they stretched out like trees, and the hours passed like the hours of a child, they did not flicker or melt deceptively away. She thought that it was not true what people said, that time passed quickly when you were happy and passed slowly when you were sad. For on her darkest days after Tarig died, grief had burned away time, devoured the hours effortlessly, the days in chunk after chunk. Now every day stretched long and when Rae spoke to her a few words, when they only saw each other for a few minutes, these minutes expanded and these words multiplied and filled up time with what she wanted to take with her, what she did not want to leave behind.

*   *   *

My last twelve days. My last ten days.

He said it was her soup, her soup was the catalyst that made him recover. He was back working a full day, he no longer coughed.

She said, 'Allah is the one who heals.' She wanted him to look beyond the causes to the First, the Real.

'When I was young,' he told her, 'there were books that did not impress me much. Picture books of Angels with blue eyes and wings, naive animals in pairs boarding a ship, too many fluffy clouds.'

When she was young there were the words of the Qur'an, no pictures of Angels. Words to learn by heart and recite in treacher-ous streets where rabid dogs barked too close. '*Say: I take refuge in the Lord of daybreak . . .*', '*Say: I take refuge in the Lord of humans . . .*' And at night too, inside the terrifying dreams of childhood, she had said the verses to push away what was clinging and cruel.

He said, 'That is real, nothing trivialised, diminished to the status of fairy-tales.' And he looked disappointed when he said that, distracted by thoughts he would only condense for her. 'History diminished to the status of fairy-tales,' he said. Covered with illusions, grid-lines, rules.

She said that she had imagined freedom in this part of the world, not rules, not restrictions. But she tried to understand, to take in this new picture he was describing. A sketch of the Scottish church and state. Calvinism, a dour and oppressive brand of Christianity. An upbringing so different from hers. Things he was told. He must not be sullen, he must not be cheeky, he must not be contra-dictory. He must not complain of boredom, only bores get bored. The value of pretending that all was well when it wasn't. Such pretence was an art, a form of courage. Don't think too much. Lighten up, you are too intense.

She said, 'I never knew that to be intense was something bad.'

'You are lucky,' he said and smiled as if he loved her. Encour-agement to speak. Again the stray dogs, the threat of rabies, cholera, bilharzia. Lepers like in films, and a day in May when the whole school was inoculated against meningitis, the injections shot out of a pistol, girls fainting in the sun. A time when she belonged to a particular place, before she knew the feeling this has nothing to do with me, these shops, these people have nothing to do with me, this sky is not for me. Times when she was silent but never detached: watching her aunt rub the luxury of Nivea on her legs, the white cream disappearing into her skin, over the sketch of bluish veins, over her ankles, the polish of her nails. Her aunt's face so serious: this was something important, necessary, not a game. 'Can I put cream on too?' But she must wash her legs first, otherwise the cream would all get mixed up with the dust. In the garden, Tarig was drinking from the hosepipe so when it was her turn she drank too. The water was warm, not cold like the water from the fridge, not smelling of food. She could drink and drink this water and never feel full. Wash her feet, her legs up to her knees. The water splashed on the mud of the flower beds, made a path into the garden. Tarig climbed the low wall, balanced. 'I fixed your bicycle,' he said. There was the sound of the water, a distant car, a few birds. There was the voice of the cook, sitting in the shade of the guava tree reading the Qur'an, his shoulders swaying back and forth with the words.

'Loneliness is Europe's malaria,' Rae said. 'No one can really be immune. This is not so hygienic a place, don't be taken in by the idols it makes of itself. You might even come to feel sorry for it, just a little, not too much, for there is no injustice in this decay. I am anxious,' he said, 'that when you go back home you will realise that I am much cruder than you, that I am not as you think me to be.'

My last Friday.

He showed her the card that his daughter sent him when he was in hospital. 'Get Well Soon, Dad', the card said and it had a picture of a bandaged bear. Sammar found the wording strange without 'I wish' or 'I pray', it was an order, and she wondered if the child was taught to believe that her father's health was in his hands, under his command. But she did not share her thoughts and instead admired the school photograph that Mhairi had sent with the card. Her uniform was a tartan kilt, a matching jumper and tie. She stood out from among the rest of her class because she was his daughter and looked a little like him.

'Whom does she resemble more, you or her mother?' Sammar asked. But he was not keen to follow this line of conversation.

Of the reasons for the break-up of his marriage, she could only guess. If she asked him directly, she knew she would not be fulfilled with the concise, measured answer he would give. So on her own she looked inside, lifted up the veils that blocked her vision. One veil: he could not make anyone unhappy: another veil: to leave him that woman must have a low IQ. Finally in the deep she caught sight of the truth: his stubbornness and a wife with a successful career who earned more money as a bureaucrat with the UN than he did as a professor in a provincial university. A woman who grew tired of travelling back and forth from Geneva to Edinburgh to see her daughter in boarding school, then to see him in Aberdeen. He would not go with her to Geneva. Geneva, he said, was too neat and for him there were only three places in the world: Scotland, North Africa, the Middle East. That woman, after a snide remark too many, *The UN is a sham and everyone knows it*, after a quarrel too many, *I spent five miserable years with you in stinking Cairo*, sat down alone one day with a coffee and a cigarette, and asked herself, 'What exactly do I need him for?'

My last Saturday. My last Sunday . . .

He phoned her but they could not speak for long. On the landing people came and went, banged the door. A girl with long greasy hairy stood behind Sammar and wanted to use the pay-phone too. Sammar wished she did not live in a place like that, she wished that she could be settled with a telephone in a kitchen that was her own. She could talk and at the same time wipe the crumbs off the table, turn the cooker off.

'I must go,' she whispered, but he would not let her go, he went on talking and she did not want to miss a single word. 'I have to go.' Behind her the girl with long hair, huffed and blew with impatience, 'Are you going to be all day? Are you going to be all day?' The girl had no mercy.

It was not the same as when she and Rae had talked a month ago, during the Christmas holidays, when Sammar had the building all to herself. Even at night, they could not talk. The stairs at night-time were dangerous highways, now and again the sounds of thumps and heaving, shouts, snatches of songs. Someone vomited on the bottom stairs, curry and beer, on the same place where Sammar had put her cushion and sat speaking to Rae.

My last Monday.

What she heard from everyone except him: *Lucky you, to get away from all this dreadful weather we've been having lately. You must be so happy you are going to see your son again. How many years since you've been back? Four years? That is a long time.*

My last Tuesday.

At that early time of the morning, the Senior Common Room was quiet. Apart from Sammar and Rae, there were two men and a lady with curly blonde hair who had slid their mugs of coffee down the metal rail to the cashier and sat under the No Smoking sign. In this room Sammar liked the tall windows that looked out over the other university buildings, the way the grass curved upwards to the road, the white dome of Engineering shaped like a mosque. Would she remember these things? The way Rae tore open a packet of sugar, would she remember that in a place where there were no packets of sugar? Or his jacket, would she remember its colour in a place where people had no need of wool or jackets? The future whined for her attention. Picture the interviews in Egypt, young men smoking one cigarette after the other. Picture sun and dusty roads, shops not so well stocked, shabby cars and shabby clothes, undecorated rooms. Picture them all, soon they will be . . .

'You are already away from me,' he said as if he could hear the future whining, as if he could see the future pulling at her hand. He watched her, he looked at her more than she looked at him. Cups of tea held her attention, smooth flawless plastic spoons.

'No. No, I'm still here.'

They were together at this uncomfortable time of the day to wring whatever time they could, what was left. In an hour they would be engulfed by work and the voices of people, they would be part of a bigger churning whole, projects for her to hurry up and finish before she left, classes for him and the visit of Dr Fareed Khalifa from Stirling. They were writing a paper together which meant hours of discussion.

She said, 'Yesterday when I spoke in Arabic to Fareed, I felt that home was close.' Yesterday, she had met him in Rae's office. He was short and energetic-looking with a beard and the habit of asking one question after the other. But she had not minded answering his questions, the curriculum vitae of her life. He had in turn told her about his wife who was a student, his three children who were in school. She had enjoyed talking in Arabic, words like insha' Allah, fitting naturally in everything that was said, part of the sentences, the vision. How many times had she over the past days said in English 'I'm leaving on Friday', and the sentence normal and natural as it was to the people who heard it, had sounded in her ears incomplete, untruthful without insha' Allah.

'You were patient with all his questions,' Rae said. 'Most people aren't.'

'You're not?'

'No.'

'Because you are secretive.'

He laughed and said, 'What makes you say that?'

She said, 'Something you said once. You and Yasmin were talking about how schoolgirls in France were not allowed to wear hijab. Do you remember? Yasmin was angry . . .'

'Yes, I remember.'

She remembered the November afternoon and feeling glad that Yasmin, who was giving her a lift home, was talking to Rae, not in any hurry to leave. Not in a hurry to go home because Nazim was off-shore and it had struck Sammar then that the three of them had no one expecting them at home, only voices that came out of radios and television sets.

She talked about that day, finding a new past that was not shrouded in sleep. A recent past that could be pulled out, silk from a drawer, to admire and touch. 'You said you liked hijab and I asked you why. It was the only thing I said the whole time . . .'

'Yasmin doesn't give you much chance to speak, does she?'

She frowned, 'That's not fair, she does . . . Anyway, I asked you why you liked it and you said because it is secretive. That is what you said.'

'And that made you think that I am secretive?'

'Yes . . .'

'I was complimenting you,' he said. 'Didn't you realise?'

She shook her head and looked out of the window at the winter sun on the dome of the Engineering building. The noise of the room, cutlery being moved, set out, the ventilator fan from the kitchen. If things were different, she would have smiled and asked, 'Complimented me on what?' and enjoyed the things he would have said. But she was afraid of confessions, emotional words. Uneasy. Meeting him, talking to him had become a need she was not comfortable with. Yesterday she had wondered if Fareed had sensed, had guessed from the way Rae looked at her, from the way she spoke. She envied Fareed because he was married and she was not, and marriage was half of their faith.

When she turned away from the window, one of the catering ladies was walking around spraying the tables with polish and wiping them with a cloth. There were more people in the room, vaguely familiar, reading newspapers, eating breakfast before they started work.

Something light to say. The tea is hot. Yasmin has a cold and she can't take anything for it because she is pregnant. Diane's mother is up from Leeds for a visit. Talk of work. Ask about his students, his best student, the man from Sierra Leone. He is finishing up his thesis. Does he have a date set for his viva, yet?

She spoke about the Azhar thesis that she was working on. She had promised him that she would finish the introduction before she left. She said, 'A lot of the hadiths that are quoted have already been translated before, so I am working faster than I thought I would be. I am learning a lot, things I didn't know before.' Here in Scotland she was learning more about her own religion, the world was one cohesive place.

'What things haven't you come across before?'

'One hadith that says, "The best jihad is when a person speaks the truth before a tyrant ruler." It is not often quoted and we never did it at school. I would have remembered it.'

'With the kind of dictatorships with which most Muslim countries are ruled,' he said, 'it is unlikely that such a hadith would make its way into the school curriculum.'

'But we should know . . .'

'The good thing,' he said, 'the balance is that you could know, that the information is there. Governments come and go and they can aggressively secularise like in Turkey, where they wiped Islam off the whole curriculum, or marginalise it like they did most everywhere else, separating it from other subjects, from history even. But the Qur'an itself and the authentic hadiths have never been tampered with. They are there as they had been for centuries. This was the first thing that struck me when I began to study Islam, one of the reasons I admire it.'

'Why did you begin to study it?'

He said, 'I wanted to understand the Middle East. No one writing in the fifties and sixties predicted that Islam would play such a significant part in the politics of the area. Even Fanon, who I have always admired, had no insight into the religious feelings of the North Africans he wrote about. He never made the link between Islam and anti-colonialism. When the Iranian revolution broke out, it took everyone here by surprise. Who were these people? What was making them tick? Then there was a rush of writing, most of it misinformed. The threat that the whole region would be swept up in this, very much exaggerated. But that is understandable to some extent because for centuries there had been a tense relationship between the West and the Middle East. Since the seventh century when the church denounced Islam as a heresy.'

Time was not generous. They looked at their watches at the same time. Only a few minutes to nine. People were leaving the room, from the window she could see students walking towards the buildings, going indoors. She said, 'What are the other reasons that you admire Islam?'

'It will have to be one reason for now, because there isn't much time. There are a number of theories,' he began and she thought, he is talking to me now like he talks to his students. She sometimes wished that she was one of his students, then she could listen to him for hours at a time.

'. . . these theories explain why capitalism developed ultimately in Europe and not in other earlier civilisations which were more sophisticated. Civilisations like Muslim Spain or the Ottoman empire. One theory is that for capitalism to grow there must be an accumulation of wealth through inheritance that comes from dynasties and families surviving over a long time. But the sharia's laws on inheritance and charity fragmented wealth so much that the necessary accumulation never took place. There was a blocking effect, like an internal thermostat or switch that stopped this excess. I think of it as a balance, something that kept things reasonable, steady. And now I have to rush because I have a class.'

After he left, she sat for a few minutes playing with the plastic spoon in her empty cup. Why was it that even though he said such positive things, she was not completely reassured. Months ago Yasmin had asked, 'Are you hoping he would become a Muslim so you could get married?' Hope that he would become, fear that he wouldn't and then what? On the table there was scattered sugar melting in tea stains, particles bouncing towards the anonymity of the carpet or staying to cling gritty and sweet on her fingers and clothes.

Her last Wednesday.

13

Her last two days.

Windows in red and blue flew towards her. They got bigger and clearer as they came close to the surface of the computer screen and then passed away. She had stopped changing Arabic into English, stopped typing; and the words had flickered and disappeared into the blackness from where the flying windows now came. From infinity, specks at first and then vibrant checks and greens.

She thought, the day after tomorrow I shall insha' Allah be on the train, Coach D, seat number 16F and by this time in the afternoon the train would have long left Scotland.

She was alone in the room because Diane had gone to her weekly Research Methods class. It was as if her presence had kept Sammar working and now she could not concentrate. She stood up and walked around. The room was small, just enough space for the two desks, two swivel chairs, Diane's *Guardian* on the floor. She looked out of the window at the parked cars, three students crossing the road, a dark freezing sky. In a few days, on another continent, sunshine all the time.

Tomorrow's goodbye weighed on her, so that now as she sat down again at the desk, she considered ways of avoiding it, bypassing the awkward words, the little silences in between. In the past when she had imagined leaving this city she had seen herself easily slipping away, casually, with nothing left behind. Now everything was murky and at times she almost forgot why she was leaving. Then she would remember Amir and feel guilty that she rarely thought of him, never dreamt of him. She was far from what her aunt wanted her to be, the child was not the focus of her life, not the centre where once his father had been.

She had no premonition about the knock on the door but she saw the sadness that came in with him. As if it were smoke, as if it had colours. Colours of ivory and mauve, faintly corrosive. Rae sat on Diane's chair. He said, 'I'm going away tomorrow,' and she became confused because she was the one who was going away, her bags were packed, her tickets crisp and new, and she became confused because this was term time and he had classes running, Fareed visiting for a few weeks.

'Do you remember I spoke to you about my uncle in Stirling?'

She nodded. She remembered him in the nursing home, the elder brother of David, who had gone to Egypt and never came back.

'He passed away . . .'

'Oh I'm sorry.'

Rae looked at the ghostly windows that blew on the computer screen. There was no tragedy in this death. But still the force of death was with them in the room, clean, irreversible. The enemy of continuity had sliced their lives today. But in this defeat there was something comforting, something soft . . .

He sat with his elbows on his knees and talked about how he had found out, the details of his uncle's last hours, the funeral ahead. And because endings inspire a looking-back, a summary, she listened to the outline of a completed life, a career, memories from a summer holiday.

He said, 'I wanted to be with you tomorrow before you left.'

'It doesn't matter.' The smoke in the room stung her eyes. This was the goodbye then, this was the goodbye she had thought she could avoid. It had come a day early.

'It matters very much. I'm so sorry.'

'Are you going to drive?' A voice with tears was not attractive. She should not talk in such an ugly voice.

'Yes, I'll drive.'

'Are you well enough to drive?'

'I'll be alright, I promise. I would hate myself if I didn't go.'

More than anything else in the world, now, she wanted to go with him to Stirling. It took her by surprise, how irrational and childish she could be. How she could want something that wasn't feasible, wasn't right at all? But she could not push the want away. More than anything else, she wanted now to leave the university, the prison of its familiar buildings, its familiar routine. She wanted to leave Aberdeen, get away from where she had been ill and sleepy for so long. They would drive south towards a city she had never been to before. They would stop on the way for petrol and from the shop he would get her mineral water and sweets.

When she spoke her voice was falsely light, wanting him to know that she was aware it could not happen, that it was frivolous, to be dismissed by common sense, dispersed with humour. 'I wish I could come with you.'

'I wish you could, it would make all the difference.'

Because he was not humouring her, because he was not surprised, she had no resistance. The sudden darkness when she covered her face with her hands, his voice and feeling his arms around her. This was what she had feared all along, that everything under the surface would converge and break. It was closer than she had imagined, prickly and sudden, noisy sobbing, messy because of her runny nose. He said he loved her, he said things that made her cry more not less. She told him that and lifted her head from his shoulder, breathed. He said sorry and held her hands, said she had beautiful hands. His hands were too warm, a little clammy, unnaturally warm as if he was not well, as if he was ill. She had not known that he was like that. She had not known this about him and now she felt sorry for him, closer to him. It was a closeness that soothed her, made her stop crying. She looked down at their fingers entwined, the difference between them and how smooth and cool her skin was.

The footsteps came like a dream. She heard them first and moved away from him, pushed her chair back. She saw the room change, shift into what it had been before: harsh neon light, paper filled, bathed in the low hum of the computer. Diane's familiar voice as she pushed open the door, 'Got some Chewies . . .', then she stopped at the unprecedented sight of her supervisor in her room, sitting on her chair. The surprise took away her usual confidence and standing before them holding her folders and books, she looked young and untidy, her cheeks red from walking in the cold.

'Hello,' said Sammar, trying to smooth out the guilt from her voice. She searched Diane's face for signs, afraid she would find suspicion. Rae was frowning, his eyes saying, 'What are you doing here?' He had forgotten that Diane too belonged to this room.

'Is it very cold outside?' Sammar asked, anything to say. Diane mumbled something about snow. The absence of a third chair meant that she stood near the door, hovering, not knowing what to do.

By that time Rae's frown had changed to understanding. He had for Diane a calm greeting, a question, 'How are you getting on with the literature review? I haven't seen anything from you lately.'

Diane mumbled that it was coming along. She was behind in her thesis and had been since the beginning of the term avoiding him. For her sake and so that the awkwardness in the room would end, Sammar wished that he would go away.

He did leave, without having explained his presence and she had to face Diane's annoyed, 'What was *he* doing here?'

While Sammar put together a reply about urgent work he needed her to do before going away, Diane dumped her books on the desk and started to empty her pockets. She reclaimed her chair, was herself again, mimicking Rae's voice, 'I haven't seen anything from you lately.' The information that he was going to Stirling caught her interest. 'That's the second time this term he gets someone to take over his classes!' she said and handed Sammar a piece of chewing gum.

It was cold when Sammar went home, a cold that had a smell, bruised her nose, stunned her mind a little. There were lights in her head, they made everything cutting, too clear for her eyes. The sight of her suitcases. They stood in the corner of the room, neat and compact. She was going away, she was already not of this room, where only a few of her things remained in their place. And she was someone else because of what he said to her today. From early on it was the way he spoke to her, to the inside of her, not around her, over her head, around her shoulders. That was how others spoke to her, their words bouncing against her skin and ears, cascading, and she perfectly still, untouched, always alone. If he would speak to her all the time, everyday. If all of life could be like that. The light in her head was too bright to see what was in the room. She couldn't see the suitcases anymore, the bed she leant against as she sat on the floor, the bottle of perfume he had given her. She couldn't see.

She would not have minded the blindness if it was not for the pain. It came from the light, it made her eyes sore, even her stomach tight. If she could forget the pain she would be calm and she would sink into the blindness with pleasing thoughts, dreaming, with the temperature falling outside. It was because Diane had come into the room. That was when the pain began, the sudden change, having to abruptly move away from him. If Diane had seen him holding her hand, if she had heard . . . It would be better not to think of that, better not to think of how, after the initial surprise, it would have looked so silly to Diane, amusing to repeat, a good piece of department gossip. If she could stop thinking of that. Gossip, tastier than average because they were an unlikely couple, because of who she was, how she dressed. Better not to think. They had been lucky, they were safe. But still the light in her head; the 'ifs' like snakes coiling, never still.

Nothing that Allah forbids His servants is good. It will only diminish them, ultimately or soon, in this life or the next. Today she had failed. Failed herself and the esteem with which he was held by others could have been threatened. The saying went, 'Only the able, clever one falls.' She had been careful all along, on her guard, and yet today had come smooth and inevitable as if it had been waiting for her all the time, close not far, close as a smile.

Seeking forgiveness from Allah. Wanting to make things right, as they should be. Only one thing could make things right, washed, clear-cut. Months ago Yasmin had asked, 'Are you hoping he would become a Muslim so you get married?' Many times Yasmin had asked 'Are you sure he is going to become a Muslim?' and Sammar had shrugged away her friend's concern, drifted along, too much in awe of what was between them to ask any questions. But now she could not go on like that. She must know, find out. She didn't even know how attached he was to his beliefs. So many things she could have asked him about and she hadn't. And now she was leaving with the future between them fluid, unsettled, her conscience troubled.

The light in her head, blurred soapy vision. A migraine like the one she had when she and Yasmin had visited him at home. It seemed a long time ago, yet it was only four months, autumn then and she had washed the mugs in the kitchen sink and looked out of the window at the lights in the other buildings, the garden at the back. She had felt welcome that day, she had felt at home and that was too much for her then, she was not strong enough and that was why the pain came.

The first part of the night passed, a bit of sleep, dreamless, light as acid. When she could see again, she saw from the window snow. Snow filled the sky and poured down like it would never stop. It covered the street below, the empty parked cars, the roofs of the buildings all around. When she was young in Khartoum and when it rained at night, thunder and lightning would wake her up, so dramatic that she used to think Judgement Day had arrived. Lightning cracking the sky like egg shell and everything covered by darkness opening out in the light.

Rain had meant an altered day, no school, flooded streets, everything in the shade. If the snow kept falling thickly, if it did not stop until morning, then the roads would be blocked. It had happened in past winters, it could happen again. Rae would not be able to go to Stirling and she could see him again, ask him and be reassured.

Maybe the roads would be blocked for days, the trains wouldn't run and even she, the day after, would not be able to leave. So much elation with this idea and the falling snow. That was what she really wanted. She did not want to go to Egypt, interpreting interviews for the anti-terrorist programme. She did not want to go to Khartoum and bring Amir, not yet, not now. How can Amir come when she was so unsettled?

If the snow would keep falling, if the roads would be blocked. She knew what she was going to do, she had the courage. Everything would be made right and simple. Already she did not belong to this room. She had finished serving time in this room: illness, convalescence, recovery. Now the room was bare and dry, lit up by the falling snow.

Dawn, and she began to put away the few of her belongings that were still not packed. Her prayer mat, a few things that were drying on the radiator, some of her folders and papers from work. The blanket, the curtains and the kitchen things went into a box that would go into storage. The bottle of perfume he had given her. She opened it and the scent was heavy enough to rise in the room, soften the edge of the cold. She thought of what she would tell him, all the things she would translate for him. He knew a lot. Like others here, this world held his attention and the scope of his mind. But he did not know about the stream of Kawthar, the Day of Promises, or what stops the heart from rusting. And the balance he admired. He would not understand it until he lived it.

Once there was a time when she could do nothing. When she was held down by something heavy. Clogged up, dragging herself to pray, even her faith sluggish. Yet Allah had rewarded her even for these imperfect prayers. She had been protected from all the extremes. Pills, break-down, attempts at suicide. A barrier was put between her and things like that, the balance that Rae admired. For this admiration she would gather her courage and talk to him. She would make him happy, she could do so much for him.

She wanted to cook for him different things, and then stand in the kitchen and think, I should change my clothes, wash, for her hair and clothes would be smelling of food. Mhairi could come and live with them, she would not need to go to boarding school anymore, and he would like that, seeing his daughter everyday, not having to drive to Edinburgh. And Mhairi would like Amir, girls her age liked younger children. She would be kind to Mhairi, she would do everything for her, clean her room, sort her school clothes. She would treat her like a princess. When they went out shopping together she would buy her pretty things, soap that smelt of raspberries and ribbons of different widths for her hair.

14

T he roads were blocked with cars that could barely move. The city's roundabouts and traffic lights were useless in the snow. So many feet of snow, the radio had announced, for so many years there had not been such heavy snow. Chaos was a rare visitor to this orderly city. It was flustered now, tense and stubborn as it insisted on following its daily rhythm. Shops must open, people must get to work. That was sacred. If Sammar had searched for anything sacred to this city and not found it, here it was. On people's faces as they pushed and scraped the snow off their cars, on the face of the bent elderly woman, miraculously still on her feet, beating the snow with her walking stick; she must get to the post office.

Over this chaos, the sun shone brighter than ever, dazzling on the white that covered the surface of things. There was sunshine like in Africa and the city slowed down, became inefficient, as if it were part of the Third World. From this came Sammar's strength. She knew this. It was familiar to her, natural and curing to the soul. She walked, her fingers frozen in spite of woollen gloves, her feet numb in her shoes. The streets were long queues of cars, awkward buses and vans. The pavements were trampled snow and patches of slippery ice. It was useless to catch a bus. The buses were elephants today.

When she got to the university, the campus was quiet without the usual busy coming and going of students. Not many cars were in the car park and the few that were there were at awkward angles and distances from each other because the snow had covered the lines of the parking spaces. Some students were playing in the snow, throwing snowballs at each other. They wore hats and colourful scarves. They were laughing, not serious and blank as they usually looked. It seemed as if there were no classes running today or only a few. The university, unlike the business world, had surrendered to the exceptional day.

Sammar met Yasmin on the steps of the building. Yasmin was visibly pregnant in spite of the large coat she was wearing. She was on her way home rather than coming in.

'There's hardly anyone in today, there's no point in me staying,' she blew her nose. 'I'm not too well. I can't get rid of this cold.'

'Is Rae here?'

Yasmin nodded, 'He's on the phone with some journalist from London . . . about the hijack.'

Sammar knew about the snow, not about a hijack. But it did not seem out of place. The whole day was different, lifted up out of the ordinary in every way.

'A Libyan Airlines on its way to Amman,' said Yasmin. 'Haven't you heard? It was on the news this morning.'

She had heard that there were power cuts in some parts of Aberdeen, the names of the schools that were closed, treacherous roads.

Yasmin said that the airplane was in Cyprus now. The hijackers wanted it refuelled but no one knew yet where they intended to go.

'Fareed was with Rae a while ago. They called Tripoli. It seems to be about freeing political prisoners in Libya. Then Fareed went to teach. I don't think more than half of his class turned up but he decided to go ahead anyway.'

Yasmin blew her nose again. It was cold standing on the steps of the building.

'You had better go,' said Sammar.

'Yes, none of the others turned up.' She meant the other secretaries.

'The roads are really bad.'

'It's good Nazim isn't off-shore,' Yasmin said. 'You're lucky you're going away. It's tomorrow, isn't it?'

'If the trains run. They cancelled them today.' Sammar stamped her feet to shake off the snow that was on her shoes.

'The airport is open. They've cleared the runway. You can get a plane to London if the trains aren't running.'

'Yes, I suppose I can.' There was no need to tell Yasmin that she did not want to go away, that she was not going away, that today everything was going to be different. But she could say insha' Allah and not feel that she was lying. She said, 'Insha' Allah tomorrow. I've packed and everything.'

They said goodbye to each other. They said they were not going to meet for a long time.

Rae was still on the telephone when she went to his office. She was content to sit and hear his voice, know that he was here, smile at him once in a while. She sat on one of the brown armchairs that made up a seating arrangement separate from his desk. On the telephone, he was speaking the way he spoke to everyone except her: cooler, quicker. Sometimes he made notes, smiled at her. He did not look sad like yesterday when he was telling her about his uncle. She was pleased about that and proud that his opinion was being asked from London, where they must have many Middle-East experts of their own.

The politics of Libya and a lot of sun in the room, hitting the shelf of books, the filing cabinet. There were labels on the filing cabinet: Research, Administration, Teaching. Her work with him came under Research. What she translated made up part of the references for the papers he published in journals, presented in conferences.

'So you didn't go to Stirling?' she said when he finished speaking on the telephone.

'I'll go in the afternoon, if the road's clear.'

She was going to ask him if he would miss the funeral when the telephone rang again. It was a colleague this time, someone he was at ease with because he laughed when he spoke of the hijack, said he was up half the night hearing the news and yes, it was nearly as good as in the seventies but unlikely to compete with Entebbe.

There were pauses when he was listening and she was unaware of what the conversation was about. She could hear the students downstairs playing in the snow. Their laughter came through the window.

A few words from Rae, snatches, 'We're having our funding cut again' . . . 'I didn't know about that' . . . 'Paris! Lucky man.'

When he finished, he said, 'I'm sorry,' and she thought of driving with him to Stirling in the afternoon. They would drive south and there would be snow piled at the side of the road. They would stop for petrol and from the shop he would get her mineral water and sweets. He left his desk and came to sit with her, leaned to kiss her but she moved her head away. His chin brushed against her scarf. They laughed a little, embarrassed now, a nervous laugh like breathing. But in the silence that followed, her resolve was strengthened. She said, 'I want to ask you something.'

'Ask me.' He was more subdued than when he was speaking on the telephone.

'I want to ask you to become a Muslim so we could . . .'

Her courage failed her. She could not look at him. She looked down at her gloves on her lap. If it could really happen, she could drive with him to Stirling to be alone with him, to be settled. The words tumbled out, 'I want to talk to you about this all the time but it's so hard. We talk of Islam when we talk of work and it's different from the way I want to talk to you.' She folded her gloves in her hands, unfolded them again.

When he didn't say anything, she looked up. If what was in his eyes was wariness, surprise, she would have felt the barriers between them, she would have withdrawn. But what she found was distress, enough to twist her with pity for him. Why, when she wanted to make him feel safe, when she wanted to look after him?

'Is the *shahadah* what you want to talk to me about?' His voice normal, the way he spoke to her.

'Yes.' She put her gloves back on.

'Are you cold?'

'No.' So much sun was in the room, but the cold was inside her. She had come with it from outside.

'There's a portable heater in the cupboard in the hall; I can get it.'

She shook her head, 'No, I'm alright.'

Somehow it was easier to talk after that, to say what she wanted to say, the way she wanted to say it. It was not difficult, confidence came.

She said, 'I wanted to talk to you about the *shahadah*, what it means.' She breathed in and went on, 'It's two things together, both beginning with the words, "I bear witness". I bear witness, I testify, to something that is intangible, invisible, but I have knowledge of it in my heart. There is no god except Allah, nothing else is worthy of worship. That's the first thing . . . Then the second thing . . . I bear witness that Muhammad is His messenger, a messenger not only to the Arabs who saw him and heard him, but to everyone, in every time.'

She thought, I have to explain things right, I have to be clear. She said, 'There were messengers before, Moses and Jesus and others. Every messenger comes with proof about himself, a miracle suitable to his time. Something that his people would find deeply impressive, something that would make them listen to him. Though even with these miracles not everyone believes.

'The Qur'an was the miracle that Muhammad, peace be upon him, was sent with. And it's different from the miracles of the other Prophets because it's still with us now . . . it's still accessible. For the Arabs who first heard it, it was something new and strange, neither poetry nor prose, something they had never heard before. When the early verses of the Qur'an were recited, many people were crying from the words and how they sounded . . .'

He said, 'Translations don't do it justice. Much is lost . . .'

'Yes, the meanings can be translated but not reproduced. And of course the miracle of it can't be reproduced . . . But even then, hearing it from the Prophet, peace be upon him, not everyone believed. Not everyone accepted that the source and wording of what they were hearing came from Allah. The first believers were mostly women and slaves. I don't know why, maybe they had softer hearts, I don't know . . .'

'Maybe in changing they did not have much to lose,' he said. 'It was the rulers of Makkah who were reluctant to give up their traditions and established ways for something new.'

She said, 'They were very bad in Makkah to the early Muslims. Muhammad was known as Al-Amin, that was what everyone called him. It means the honest, the trustworthy, but when he said, "I am a messenger from Allah", he was called liar, mad-man, poet. These are the doubts that people have . . . Allah tells us in the Qur'an, reminds us again and again, these verses are not the words of a poet, they are Divine revelation, certain truth.'

She paused and then said, 'Everything in my religion comes from this. The words of the Qur'an which you told me the seventh-century Pope dismissed as heresy . . . Now tell me if you believe or not.'

*   *   *

She walked to the window. Flakes of snow drifted down from the roof, talcum powder, icing sugar. She saw the students whose voices she had been hearing. They were in the car park, two boys rolling a huge snowball grey with dirt from the ground. They laughed as they propped it against the door of one of the cars. She felt old looking at them; they were young and did not have many responsibilities. If Rae said no, what exile would he put himself in? If he said no, she would walk out on to the snow, an exile she would take with her wherever she went.

When she turned around he said, 'I am not sure.'

She had expected yes or no. She would have known what to say if he had said yes. She would have known what to do if he had said no.

She sat down and because she was silent he repeated, 'I'm not sure.'

She said, 'Do you know what it means for us?'

'I know. I've always known.'

'I imagined we could get married today.' Her voice startled and bruised her, like sandpaper, like sea-salt. 'Now, and I could go with you to Stirling. I don't want to go to Egypt.'

'How could we get married now?' The same distress in his voice.

'I thought Fareed could marry us and it would not be difficult to get two witnesses.' She had imagined students as witnesses. Even with the snow, they could still have found Muslim students. It was not how she had got married to Tarig, but it was how it used to be when people lived by Islam alone. Two witnesses, and a gift. A gift however simple or small. In the Prophet's time, two chapters of the Qur'an were an acceptable gift from a man who had nothing to give his new wife but verses which he had memorised. Now in Muslim countries, it was gold and dollar bills, endless discussions about who should buy the video set and fridge-freezer.

There was a silence in the room. She thought, why isn't he

saying anything, why isn't he talking to me? She thought, why am I numb, why am I not crying yet?

'I thought you were homesick,' he finally said, 'and this anti-terrorist project would be a chance for you to go on to Khartoum, see your son. Maybe I made a mistake in suggesting it . . .'

'It wasn't a mistake. I was homesick for the place, how every-thing looked. But I don't know what kind of sickness it would be, to be away from you.'

He said, 'I know what my sickness would be . . .'

'Don't say no then, not sure is better than no, don't ever say no.'

'It's not in me to be religious,' he said. 'I studied Islam for the politics of the Middle East. I did not study it for myself. I was not searching for something spiritual. Some people do. I had a friend who went to India and became a Buddhist. But I was not like that. I believed the best I could do, what I owed a place and people who had deep meaning for me, was to be objective, detached. In the middle of all the prejudice and hypocrisy, I wanted to be one of the few who was saying what was reasonable and right.'

'It's not enough,' she pressed her hands together. 'It's not enough. It's not enough for me.'

He leaned and put his elbows on his knees, his face in his hands.

She said, 'Don't you realise how much you hurt me saying objective and detached, like you are above all of this, above me, looking down . . .'

'No, no it isn't . . .' His face had a deeper colour as if he had pressed it too hard against his hands.

'It is. It is looking down, saying it has nothing to do with you, not for you. When you know very well that it's for everyone. You know it's not just for Arabs. You know the *figures*, you know more than me how much percentage are Chinese, Russians . . .'

'I didn't say it has nothing to do with me. I didn't say that.'

'You're not reassuring me, you're not saying anything to stop me being anxious.' She was shivering. If she did not hold her teeth together they would start chattering.

'You're cold,' he said. 'This room can get too cold.'

She nodded. All the sunshine in the room, the light laughter coming up through the window and no warmth.

'I'll go get the heater from the cupboard,' he said.

His absence was harsh, abrupt. In his absence the room was bleak, filled with too many things: books, papers, a telephone that rang only for him. She sat where his students sat, on that same armchair, panicking about their exams, their financial difficulties, on the edge of dropping out. She imagined that he was reasonable with them, genuinely concerned. It occurred to her now that she had come here to his office to ask him to marry her and he had not said yes. He had not said yes, and yet here he still sat, clinging. She had no pride. If she had pride she would go away now. Instead she was still sitting.

He came back pulling a large heater on wheels. It took time for him to untangle the wire, plug the socket in the wall. His movements were slow, a little clumsy, someone who did not spend much time doing things with his hands.

The rods on the heater glowed pink and orange. When he sat down he said, 'Be patient with me, I don't know what to do . . . All this fumbling and I never had so much empathy for anyone in my life.'

She did not understand the meaning of the word 'empathy'. At times he did say words she could not understand, words she would ask him to explain. Sixties' scene, Celtic, chock-a-block. But now she did not ask him the meaning of 'empathy'. Today she could not ask. It sounded like 'sympathy', and, she thought, he feels sorry for me. To him I must have always looked helpless and forlorn.

Somehow she was able to speak, make the last attempt, 'If you say the *shahadah* it would be enough. We could get married. If you just say the words . . .'

'I have to be sure. I would despise myself if I wasn't sure.'

'But people get married that way. Here in Aberdeen there are people who got married like this . . .'

'We're not like that. You and I are different. For them it is a token gesture.'

She thought, it is clear now, it is so clear, he does not love me enough, I am not beautiful enough. I am not feminine enough coming here to ask him to marry me when I should have waited to be asked.

'Why did you talk to me then? From the beginning, why did you start all this. You should have just left me alone. You had no right. If you were content in your religion . . .'

'I'm not content, there are too many things I can't justify to myself. Of course I'm not content. Isn't it obvious to you?'

'Nothing is obvious to me.' Nothing except that she was rubbing her pride back and forth over barbed wire.

'I wish I never trusted you,' she said and saw pain in his eyes. 'What did you *imagine* all this was going to lead to?'

'I imagined a longer time before . . .'

'From the beginning, you should have looked at me and said, she is not for me.'

'No, I couldn't.' He put his face in his hands, pressed his eyes and forehead.

She said, 'Yes, that would have been the sensible thing. Objective and detached, you say. So what do you need from me?' She had tried to make her voice sound sarcastic, cool and sarcastic but is sounded twisted and childish.

He did not look at her, he continued to sit with his head in his hands. If he had looked at her she might have stopped talking. But there was nothing to check her.

'I'm not fooled by you. Just because you were kind to me and paid me attention. That's all. But you would have always been second best . . . And I don't want to live here for the rest of my life with this stupid weather and stupid snow. Do you know what I wish for you? Do you know what I'm going to pray and curse you with. I'm going to pray that if it's not me then it's no one else and you can live the rest of your life alone and miserable. There really must be something wrong with you to have been divorced *twice*, not once, but twice . . .'

It was a sound that stopped her, a movement of his shoulders. It frightened her. Because his head was in his hands, she thought he was crying. She thought she had hurt him enough to make him cry. For a second there was triumph, the crazy happiness of thinking, he does love me, good, he is not immune to me.

She walked towards him to put her hand on his shoulders, to say, don't cry. She did not stop when he mumbled, 'Go away.' She did not hear him clearly when he said, 'Get out of here.'

Only when he looked at her. Not crying, she had been wrong about that, but looking at her in a way he had never looked at her before. His voice different than the way he always spoke to her. She heard him clearly this time when he said, 'Get away from me.'

She obeyed him. She turned and picked up her bag from the floor. She found the door knob, she opened the door, left the room without looking back. Down the steps, out of the building, to the sunshine and the snow. Everything clear and cold. Her breath smoke, the snow speckles of diamonds to step on.

15

S he obeyed him. She went home and telephoned a taxi to take her to the airport. She carried her suitcases downstairs, knocked on Lesley's door for the key to the basement to store the boxes she was not taking with her.

The taxi ride to the airport was slow but the traffic was moving, not at a stand-still as it had been earlier in the day. At the airport they put her on a waiting list. The morning flights to London had been delayed and there was a back-log of people waiting. But one seat to London, either Heathrow or Gatwick, she stood a good chance, they said, of leaving before tonight.

It was a plush, clean airport, crowded today with oil-men on their way to Shetland, women with small children, men in business-suits. Sammar's eyes missed nothing. She could see everything, register everything. Her mind would not think, would not dwell or settle on anything. Just her vision, so much to look at, everything gritty bright.

Airport shops. Sweets for Amir. Something Scottish for Hanan.

Hunger, acute hunger. A long queue at the cafeteria. Vegetable lasagna, very good, a lot of gooey cheese, white sauce. Chocolate cake. Cappuccino.

Going to the toilet. Her face in the mirror, not pleasing, but there was no surprise in that. Wash her hands. I don't like the smell of this soap. Press a knob and warm air rushes out. Modern technology.

She sat on a green seat reading the information on the screen, Arrivals, Departures, reading it again and again. Feeling the sun outside the window wane. Time to pray and the sadness that there was nowhere to pray in the airport. If she stood up and prayed in the corner, people would have a fit. A story once told by Yasmin: Turks in London praying in Terminal 1 and someone called the police.

Sammar prayed where she was, sitting down, not moving.

In a few hours she would leave. Get away. Get away. Get out of here.

The clock on the wall. Twenty-four hours ago, she did not even know that Rae's uncle had died. Twenty-four hours ago. Enough to break the mind. Don't think. Just look around, open your eyes wide.

Time to board. The early darkness of winter. Outside the double-glazing of the terminal, freezing gusts of air . . . walking up the metal steps to the airplane. Smiling stewardesses, too much make-up, handing her the evening paper. Navy seats, the characteristic smell of airplanes, the fumble with overhead lockers.

Fasten seat-belts. British Airways' policy of no smoking on its domestic flights.

On the front page of the paper, a picture of the hijacked airplane on the tarmac at Cyprus. Today's date written on the paper. Today Thursday. Tomorrow was the day she was meant to leave. Just tomorrow. There was really no drama in this flight. No one will notice that she had gone. She had wasted her money on an airline ticket, wasted the train ticket she had for tomorrow. But he had said get away, get out of here.

Take-off, the roar of take-off, the running, running leap into the air. The airplane rose up over the city. In the twilight, the world below was splashed with snow. Sammar looked out of the window and saw miniature houses, cars and trees; the pale frothy sea. Small, compact city that belittled her hope.

PART TWO

. . . the fog cleared and I awoke, on the second day of my arrival, in my familiar bed in the room whose walls had witnessed the trivial incidents of my life in childhood and the onset of adolescence . . . I heard the cooing of the turtle-dove, and I looked through the window at the palm tree standing in the courtyard of our house . . . I looked at its strong straight trunk, at its roots that strike down to the ground, at the green branches hanging down loosely over its top, and I experienced a feeling of assurance. I felt not like a storm-swept feather but like that palm tree, a being with a background, with roots . . .

Tayeb Salih (1969)

16

S he wore sunglasses now. They darkened the blue of the sky, the building that had sprung up in the once empty square in front of her aunt's house. A cooperative which in working hours filled the road with noise and parked cars. Her glasses tinted the garden blue, its patches of dry yellow, the Disney characters on the children's paddling pool. She had straightened up the sides of the pool and put it in the shade, filled it with water that gushed from the hosepipe hot. Two hours before sunset and the sun was a spot of blue heat, still too piercing for eyes that had seen fog and snow. Sammar sat on the porch near the old cactus plants in their clay pots, bougainvillea in dimpled mud. Children's voices and laughter. The sight of them. They were in their underwear: Amir's pants sagging with water, Dalia's white, clinging and transparent, and the twins, Hassan and Hussein, in striped red and green. They had soaked the grass around the pool and it was now mud and slush, flat in the shade of the eucalyptus tree.

Behind Sammar the house was sleeping, hummed by fans and air coolers. Siesta before sunset and the time for praying and tea, going out or visitors parking their cars on the pavement outside. Her aunt's house was a busy house, a lot of coming and going, snapping open the tops of Miranda bottles, boiling water for tea, special trays for guests, an elegant sugar bowl. Hanan lived on the top floor with her husband and four children. Sammar had known Dalia, who was the same age as Amir, but she had seen the two-year-old twins only in photographs. And of course the baby was new, asleep now with Mahasen downstairs. Sammar sat on the porch and there was no breeze, no moisture in the air, all was heat, dryness, desert dust. Her bones were content with that, supple again, young. They had forgotten how they used to be clenched. Her skin too had darkened from the sun, cleared and forgotten wool and gloves. She waited for everything else to forget: the inside of her and her eyes. Her eyes had let her down, they were not as strong as they had been in the past, not as strong as the eyes of those who had not travelled north. She must shield them with blue lenses and wait for them to forget like her bones had forgotten and her skin. She wanted to pick up life here again. People smile when I come into a room and this tree is for me, this scrawny garden, this sun. These children are all mine, the one I carried inside me and the ones I did not.

No one will tell me get out of here, get away, get away from me.

'Sammar, Sammar': it was the neighbour's daughter calling from across the wall. Sammar walked across the porch, down the steps towards the car-port. There was a tap and a sink on the floor with a raised cement edge. Standing on it she could talk to Nahla who was standing on the arms of a chair. Two days ago, in this same position, Nahla had lost her balance and fallen. She was undeterred though and now shook hands with Sammar and kissed her over the wall.

'If you fall again, you'll break and be in bandages at the wedding.' Nahla was getting married next month. She was beautiful, with dimples and dark-coloured veils that never slipped off her hair, rectangular gauze falling at each side of her face, balancing somehow without the aid of a pin or a broach.

'I'm not going to fall off. Last time I had these stupid sandals on and they made me slip'.

'What are you wearing now?'

'I'm barefooted. Bring the children and come over.'

'I can't. They're swimming.'

'Where?'

'I got them this paddling pool when I came. Aunt Mahasen wanted me to get roller blades for Amir but I got the pool instead. I've been here a month and only got round to filling it up for them today. Come and see them. They look nice.'

In a few minutes Nahla was admiring the paddling pool. She took off her sandals, lifted her skirt and waded in, adding to the children's excitement. Amir leaned on the side and the water started spilling out.

'Stop it, Amir. You're getting rid of all the water.' Nahla took hold of his arm and pulled him but he wriggled free, his ribs showing and his knees covered with scars from cuts and mosquito bites.

Sammar got the hose to add to the water in the pool. She sprayed Amir and Dalia and they squealed and ran out of the pool across the garden, the ribbon in Dalia's hair wet and falling over her shoulders. Hassan got water on his face and he started to splutter and gasp, his hair wet curls covering his brow.

'I'm sorry, my love.' Sammar put the hose down and wiped his bewildered face. He wasn't crying and soon went back to his game of filling a cup with water and pouring it over the side of the pool.

'Sammar, come in, the water's nice. I don't feel so hot now.'

'No, I'm too old.' She smiled and turned to spray the dust off the jasmine bushes that lined the border of the garden.

'You're not old,' said Nahla. 'Haven't you seen Hanan?' Nahla puffed out her cheeks and did an exaggerated waddle from one side of the pool to the other.

Sammar laughed, looking to check that Dalia hadn't noticed

they were speaking about her mother. It was true though. Hanan did look matronly and walked as if she was still pregnant. 'It's just because of the baby,' she said, putting down the hose to water the flower beds. 'She'll become slim soon especially now she is back to work.' Hanan was a dentist.

'She was like that even before the baby, you didn't see her. No, you look years younger than her.'

Sammar took off her glasses. The sunlight was startling white, ruthless. She wiped water off the lenses with the hem of her blouse. Compliments on her looks hardened her inside. What was the use?

'How's your mother now?' she asked. Nahla's mother was ill with malaria. Yesterday Sammar and Mahasen had gone to visit her.

'*Al hamdulillah*, she's up today. Lots better. But I'm afraid all the preparations for the wedding will tire her,' she kicked the water, made little waves. 'Our luck isn't very good.'

'Why not?'

'The Syrian club is booked on the day we want.'

'Try another club.'

'The Syrian is the best, so we might change the date.' Nahla bent down and started playing with the twins' cups and beakers, showing them how to pour from one to the other.

'I haven't been to a wedding for ages,' said Sammar. 'Yours will be the first.'

'Didn't you go to weddings in Scotland?'

'No.'

Nahla looked at her with wide, kohl-rimmed eyes, 'Why not?'

'I didn't know many people there. Sometimes I saw wedding couples outside churches having their photographs taken. They don't get married like us at home. They get married in church or . . .'

'Yes, I've seen them in films.' Nahla didn't seem interested in how people got married in other parts of the world, 'I hope your aunt Mahasen will come to my wedding.'

'I don't know. Has she been going to weddings?'

'No, not since Tarig,' Nahla paused, 'Allah, have mercy on him.'

'Allah, have mercy on him,' Sammar repeated. 'Even if Aunt Mahasen doesn't go to the party at the club she'll come to the *agid* at your house.'

Nahla stepped out of the pool splashing her sandals with water. Pretty ankles, painted toenails, all the preparations for a bride. Sammar was like that once, years ago, years ago before Scotland, before Tarig died.

Here in this house, in this language and this place, were all the memories. All that had been taken away from her. A photograph of Tarig when she had walked into the house for the first time. Smiling, sitting back in a chair, at ease with everything. So young. So young and confident compared to her. He did not know her anymore. The young man in the photograph did not know the Sammar who had lived alone in Aberdeen. The photograph made her cry, tears coming from the fatigue of the journey, the strain of the past weeks in Egypt, the excitement of seeing Amir again, and he so cool, accepting her hugs and kisses as he would from the many visitors and relations who crossed his life. When she cried her aunt and Hanan started to cry. Hanan feeding the baby, sniffing into a tissue, Mahasen still and straight-backed, her tears falling without her face crumpling, without the indignity of sobbing. Only after they had cried together did the awkwardness of their meeting begin to break, the years she was away. Only then was it as if reaffirmed that she was who she was, Amir's mother, Tarig's widow coming home.

She walked Nahla to the gate, then it was time to get the children out of the pool, take them indoors, give them showers. The bathroom was so hot that she dripped with sweat while they dripped with water. Soap and squeals. 'You put soap in my eyes!', screams, guilt, Hassan's blood-shot accusing eye, his slippery arm beating against her skirt, 'Bad Sammar, ugly Sammar.'

Talcum powder and fresh clothes. 'I'm not wearing this,' Dalia folded her arms across her chest with all the authority of her mother.

'Why not, it's lovely. This is a lovely rabbit.'

'It's ugly.'

'Amir, do you think it's ugly?'

'No.'

'See, Amir thinks it's lovely and Mama when she wakes up will think it's lovely and Grandma Mahasen . . .'

'I want to wear the red one.'

'The red one is in the washing; it's dirty.'

'I *want* the red one.'

'You can't wear the red shirt. Wear the rabbit one and I'll take you out with me and Amir this evening.'

'Where are you going?'

Sammar pulled the rabbit T-shirt over Dalia's head. There was no resistance. The child pushed her arms through the sleeves and looked at Sammar expectantly.

'We're going to Uncle Waleed's house.'

Dalia frowned. She could not remember who Uncle Waleed was.

'My brother,' said Sammar. 'Remember, they have a balcony with birds in a cage.' She smoothed Dalia's eyebrows, ruffled by water and the neck of the T-shirt. 'Let's get out of this heat,' she said and pulled the bathroom door open, glad to get out of the stuffiness into the coolness of the hall.

The hall led to the sitting room, where the television and the big air cooler was. There was two beds along the wall and three old armchairs. There were stools for the children to sit on and a low circular coffee table made of light wood, which wobbled and swayed but still served as a dinner table, and for the homework

Amir and Dalia did every afternoon. The house had another sitting room, the *sallown* as everyone called it. It was for formal guests, a lifeless room, not for everyday use. Sammar had received some of her friends there when they had come to welcome her back. She had sat with them conscious of a wedding photograph of her and Tarig, she as a bride looking ignorant and young. 'Don't you think it is better to take down that photograph from the *sallown*?' she had asked her aunt and was answered with a look of suspicion, a quick no. And Mahasen must have complained to Hanan, for the next day Hanan said, 'My mother still can't get over it. Sammar, please, for Allah's sake, don't annoy her. He was her only son.'

Her only son. It was like that from the day she had brought Tarig home, carried in an airplane, in a box. Her only son. The words on everyone's lips, said in disbelief, Mahasen's son died, Mahasen's son died. Her only son. He left an orphan. Poor orphan. My heart is breaking over this orphan boy. My heart is breaking over Mahasen, her only son. It was like that from the day Sammar brought Tarig home from Aberdeen and she the one who was carrying failure, her life ripped, totally changed, losing aim, losing focus, while Mahasen and Hanan went on as before and Amir could not miss the father he could not remember.

In the sitting room, her aunt was awake but the baby was still asleep on the bed between the wall and Mahasen's back. In spite of the grief that had aged her aunt's face, there was still an elegance about her, something refined in the way she sat and the way she talked. She was watching a video with the children. A cat chased a mouse on the screen, forever frustrated, forever unfulfilled. Sammar greeted her aunt and sat on one of the stools to comb Dalia's hair. If she didn't comb it and braid it now while it was wet, it would frizz up and be impossible to untangle. The wide-toothed comb was slippery in her hands. 'Aw,' said Dalia, her concentration still on the screen.

'Sorry, pretty one. I'm nearly finished. Do you want two braids or one?'

'Two.'

Mahasen said, 'Two suits her better. Tighten them, last time you made them too loose and they didn't last.'

Sammar nodded, parted Dalia's hair in the middle and started to braid it. She could feel her aunt watching her. If she turned away now from Dalia's hair and looked up at her aunt, she would meet her eyes, see the expression on them. Something like disappointment or disapproval, a kind of contempt. Many times when she met her aunt's eyes she found that contempt when once, years ago, there was approval and love. 'I love your mother more than I love you,' she used to tease Tarig years ago. Another time, before the lines of defeat on Mahasen's face, her faded eyes.

Sammar concentrated on Dalia's hair and did not look up at her aunt. Even though the air cooler was blowing she still felt hot. She lifted her arm and with the sleeve of her blouse wiped the sweat that fell over her forehead.

'Why are you so dishevelled today?' Her aunt's voice different than the chatter and music of the cartoon show.

'I was with the children in the garden. They played with the pool. Nahla came over.' Politeness required that she looked up. She lowered her eyes again.

'Insha' Allah they're not going to have the wedding party in the house. Loud music and crowding the whole street.'

'No, she told me they're booking the Syrian club.' She was going to add that Nahla was hoping Mahasen would attend, but decided against it.

'I have no appetite for weddings or parties,' her aunt said as if she could read her mind, 'from the day they buried the deceased, I have no appetite for such things. Hanan goes, reluctantly, but it's her duty to go. It's expected of her.'

'Yes,' said Sammar. She did not like her aunt saying 'the

deceased', never referring to Tarig by his name. It made him sound as if he was old when in reality he was young, forever young. Nor did she believe that Hanan went to parties 'reluctantly'. But she kept silent as she finished Dalia's hair and did not contradict her aunt, did not look up. Over the hum of the air cooler, over the music of the cartoon show, she heard from a distance the sunset azan. She had missed it in Aberdeen, felt its absence, sometimes fancied she heard it in the rumble of the central-heating pipes, in a sound coming from a neighbouring flat. It now came as a relief, the reminder that there was something bigger than all this, above everything. *Allah akbar. Allah akbar* . . .

She went to make *wudu* and had to tidy the bathroom first because the children had splashed the walls with water, thrown towels and wet clothes on the floor. In the bedroom she put on the ceiling fan and picked up the prayer mat that lay folded on her aunt's bed. Sammar's clothes and belongings were in a separate room which had locked cupboards and crates of Miranda, sacks of sugar and rice, but she slept in this room with her aunt and Amir. Electricity was too expensive to keep more than one air cooler going throughout the night. That was why they had to share the room, share the one air cooler. Sometimes there were power cuts during the night and the sudden silence of the air cooler would wake Sammar up. She would turn its switch to Off, because sometimes the surge of the power coming back was too strong and likely to damage the motor. Sometimes she fell asleep again in the remaining coolness of the room but minutes later the heat would wake her up. She would open all the windows but sometimes not even a breeze would enter the stifling room. Amir would toss and push the cover away from him, her aunt would sit up and lean against the wall, sighing curses at the government, the electricity company, life itself. And Sammar would get up and go outside, pace up and down the star-lit porch, unsteady from lack of sleep, stunned by the laden sky. In the past everyone had slept outdoors on the roof, wide-open space, a freshness even on the hottest nights. But Hanan had built her flat on the roof. '*No one*, Sammar,' she said, 'sleeps outdoors anymore.' Because of mosquitoes bred by open drains and fumes of diesel rising during power cuts from bright houses that could afford generators.

After she prayed she went out to the garden. It was different without the children and she did not need her sunglasses now. She could have all the colours that she had missed in Aberdeen; yellow and brown, and everything else vivid. Flat land and a peaceful emptiness, space, no grey, no wind, no lines of granite. The sun had rimmed the houses down the road and left behind layers of pink and orange. In the east there was the confident blue of night, a flimsy moon, one, two, now three stars. Still the birds rushed to the trees, screeching, rustling the leaves, noisier than the children had been earlier on. On the other side of the road, the night-watchman of the cooperative was serving his friends tea. They sat on the pavement on a large palm-fibre mat; prayer beads and laughter. Coals glowed, a kettle of water boiled and let off steam in the twilight. Her homesickness was cured, her eyes cooled by what she saw, the colours and how the sky was so much bigger than the world below, transparent. She heard the sound of a bell as the single, silly light of a bicycle lamp jerked down the pitted road. A cat cried out like a baby and everything without the wind had a smell; sand and jasmine bushes, torn eucalyptus leaves.

17

Her brother Waleed lived with his wife in a second-floor flat in one of the newer apartment blocks. They were newly married and both worked for the same architecture office. Sammar parked Hanan's car under the dim yellow glow of a street lamp. The driving lessons she had taken in Aberdeen had come in useful after all, though at first the change to driving on the right was difficult. Amir and Dalia opened the car door and jumped out. 'If we were in Scotland,' she said to them as they crossed the road, 'you would have had to sit in the back and wear seat-belts.' What she said made no sense to them. They had never seen anyone wear a seat-belt; they could not imagine a place far away called Scotland.

The road they walked across was pitted with potholes, strewn with rubble from the new buildings. Bricks and scattering of cement were everywhere, the playthings of children who lived on the streets. There was a small canteen next to the building and some of the children were crowded near the entrance. They were in torn stained clothes, bare feet covered with dust up to their ankles. They wanted lollipops and gum, and were laughing and jostling each other, their teeth bright white in the poorly lit street. And though Sammar had come back from rain and a rich city of the First World, the meagerness of this place was familiar. Shabbiness as if the sun had burned away the lushness of life and left no room for luxuries or lies.

As soon as Waleed opened the door for them, the power failed. There was much confusion in the sudden dark with Amir jumping about in a state of great excitement, laughing and calling Dalia names because she was afraid. There was a fumble for candles and a torch, attempts to soothe Dalia, a joke about Sammar cutting off the electricity, bringing in the darkness with her.

Waleed led them through the flat and out to sit on the balcony. This pleased the children who started to pester the pigeons asleep inside a large crate caged with mesh. They stuck their fingers through the holes in the mesh, trying to reach the pigeons. All the neighbouring houses and roads were in darkness, proof of a major power cut and not a fault in the building. Only far away shone the lights of the airport, yellow and red. In the canteen below, someone lit a hurricane lamp and a shout in the street was answered by laughter. There was enough light from the moon and the stars for Sammar to see her brother clearly, the *jellabia* he was wearing, the large gap between his teeth when he smiled. He said that his wife had gone to her German lesson.

'Why is she learning German?' asked Sammar, her mind on the stars, that they were innumerable, some further away than others. How could this be the same sky as the one in Aberdeen?

'Do you think *I* know?' he said. 'She wants to learn German, what can I say, don't learn German?'

'I thought she was doing computing in Souk Two.' Everyone could look up at this sky, no admission fee, no money. In Scotland there were shops for everything, selling everything and no one could buy a sky like that.

'She was, but there weren't enough computers to go round and she didn't get much chance on the machines. She got the notes and she can use the one we have here . . .'

'Actually I want to use your computer today,' Sammar said, 'I need to write a letter, two really. But now there's no electricity.' She turned to Amir and Dalia, 'Stop it you two, leave the birds alone.' Amir banged the mesh with his palms. One of the pigeons stirred but did not wake up.

'Insha' Allah it will come back. Yesterday it was out at this time and back after fifteen minutes.'

'That would be good.' She wondered why she did not care so much about the power cut, why she was not annoyed with this obstacle. Usually she liked getting things over with once she had reached a decision. Perhaps it was because of the sky and the breeze, dewy and clear. Or the feeling all around of surrender. The stars had mocked the lights of the earth and won.

'What were you doing before we came?' she asked.

'Watching a video.' He scratched his head and yawned.

'Remember in the past we used to go to the cinema a lot.'

'No one goes to the cinema now.' By 'no one' he meant his circle of friends and family.

'It's a shame.'

'Things change. You want to go away and come back and find everything the same?'

She shrugged in the dark. There was always a tone in his voice that seemed to her harsh. But she knew he didn't mean it. She was the one who had become too sensitive. She was the one who had been away for too long.

'I want to get away from here,' he suddenly said. 'I'm fed up. I'm truly fed up.'

'Of what?' her voice was light as if she wanted to dilute his resentment.

'Not going forward. Things just aren't moving ahead.'

'Where do you want to go?'

'The Gulf or Saudi Arabia. The Gulf preferably.'

'Go.'

He laughed, 'Don't be stupid. Everyone wants to go there and make themselves a bit of money; it's not so easy.' He was genuinely amused, shaking his head, looking into her eyes, 'You have no idea, do you? You're blank.'

She started to laugh too and looked up at the stars, 'I'm blank.'

Dalia came and leaned close to her, whispered in her ears, 'I want to pee.'

The bathroom was hot and airless. In the mirror over the sink, Sammar saw her face by candlelight. How long would it be before she started to look as she should look, a dried-out widow, a faded figure in the background?

'I've finished,' Dalia said. Sammar had to yank the toilet handle three times before it finally flushed. Dalia's anxious face settled into a smile and Sammar noticed that the cistern did not fill up again with water. 'It must be that when the electricity cuts, the pump that lifts the water up to this floor stops working. Let's try the taps.'

Dalia twisted the tap. A few drops spluttered out noisily and then there was nothing.

'They've got a pail . . .' said Sammar. There was a pail full of water in the bathtub and a metal pitcher. She filled the pitcher with water and Dalia washed her hands in the sink, the white bar of soap large and awkward in her hand.

They walked back carefully through the darkness, Sammar carrying the candle, to the coolness of the balcony. In their absence Waleed had brought a tray of Pepsi bottles and glasses with ice, plates of peanuts and dates.

Amir and Dalia were soothed by the drinks, made silent by the peanuts. Sammar shook the ice in her glass. It was one of the things she had missed in Aberdeen, ice cubes in drinks, the feel of a cool drink in the heat.

'So what do you think of this dark country of ours?' Waleed asked putting his hands behind his head. He meant the power cut.

'Beautiful.'

He laughed. His laugh was loud and contagious.

'At last you've gone mad,' he said in between his laughter.

She smiled and said slowly, 'I swear by Allah Almighty, I see it more beautiful than anywhere else.' Because she had mentioned Allah her heart glowed and because she spoke the truth.

'I'll give you a couple more weeks,' he said, 'you'll take Amir and run back.'

She shrugged. 'I'm not going to have a job to go back to. I'm here today to write my letter of resignation and send it off.'

'Why are you going to do that?' It was almost a yell. He sat forward in his chair, intense now, no longer laughing, 'You must never do that. Do you think jobs are lying about waiting for people to pick them up? Do you think you're going to find a job here?'

'I'll just have to try, Insha' Allah I'll find something.' She flicked away some peanut husks that had fallen on her lap and wished she hadn't told him. If his wife had been at home, he would have been more subdued, not so hyped-up. Now he went on and on.

'What sort of work do you think you're going to find?'

'Maybe the "Erasing Illiteracy" programme . . .'

'The pay will be nothing, nothing you could live on, you'll just regret it. And you've never taught before . . .'

'They're desperate for people, they won't fuss . . .'

'Yes, they won't fuss, but *why,* when you have a very good job already in Aberdeen, *why* give up a chance?'

'I was supposed to be back at work last week. They're probably wondering what happened to me.'

'That's not a reason to resign.'

She looked into her glass, melting ice, dark-golden Pepsi, 'Living there wasn't a great success.'

'How couldn't it be? You're so fortunate. A good job, a civilised place. None of there power cuts and strikes and what not . . . What's the matter with you?'

'I don't know.'

'Just like that.'

'Just like that.' There was guilt in her voice, a kind of stubbornness. She could see the irony of the situation. She had the option of a life abroad and wanted to stay, while he was keen to leave and couldn't.

She said as if to explain, 'Being exiled isn't very nice.'

'If you took Amir with you, you wouldn't be lonely and it would be good for him. You don't know how schools here have become.'

'I wouldn't be able to handle him on my own.' She wished she could explain how desolate it would be, her and Amir alone in Aberdeen. The long winter evenings, the small room they would live in, just them, the two of them, face to face, claustrophobic.

'That's rubbish. Here you're handling Amir *and* Hanan's children. Didn't Aunt Mahasen fire the maid as soon as you came back?'

Sammar laughed relieved at the turn in the conversation. Waleed smiled reluctantly. She said, 'No one fired anyone. The woman left, she just disappeared a week after I came back. And Aunt Mahasen hasn't been able to find anyone else.'

'Oh really,' he said with sarcasm, 'Aunt Mahasen and Hanan put together couldn't find anyone.'

'I don't mind,' she said, 'I truly don't mind.' The housework and Hanan's children kept her busy, tired her out so that there was no time to dream at night.

'How has she been with you?' His voice was cautious now, the question tentative. If his wife had been at home he would not have asked.

'Fine.'

'You know that she kicked 'Am Ahmed out of the house?'

Sammar shook her head, bit her lip. It was all her fault. He didn't deserve that. She wondered how many people knew the whole story, almost a scandal. The elderly religious man, already married with two wives, setting his eyes on a young widow, her husband not yet a year in his grave. And the foolish girl did not turn him down straightaway. Instead she said she would consider it. An educated girl like her!

'What happened?' Her voice was quiet with reluctance, as if she didn't really want to know.

Waleed shifted in his chair. 'He came for a visit. I was there. It was the Eid, some time after you left. We were all just sitting there normally then Mahasen suddenly turned on him and shouted, don't ever set foot in my house again; Tarig's wife will never be yours . . . And on and on.'

'Oh my Lord.'

'Yes, it was unpleasant. We went and apologised to him later, me and Hanan. He was staying with his brother in Safia.'

'Hanan never told me about this.'

'There's no need. The whole matter is finished. I think he doesn't come to Khartoum so often now. Business isn't what it used to be. I've lost touch with him. He was cordial enough with us when we went to apologise, but things can't be the same again.'

'He's a good person,' she said. He was a life-long family friend. When she was young, he used to lift her up to sit on top of his van, he used to give her sweets. She was never afraid of him.

'What he did was an exaggeration.' Waleed's tone was dismissive.

She didn't say anything and he went on, 'I was just concerned with how Aunt Mahasen is with you. If you're comfortable living with her. Especially if you're insisting on not going back to Aberdeen.'

'She never speaks about what happened. As for living with her, Amir and I both have a share in the house. It's our right to be there.' At one time the house was shared between Mahasen, Hanan and Tarig. After Tarig's death Mahasen's share increased, Hanan's remained the same, Sammar inherited a share and to Amir went the biggest portion. The biggest in comparison to the others, but it was less than half of the house. None of them had the cash to buy the others out. If they sold the house and divided the money, it would not be enough for each of them to get a decent place elsewhere.

'It's not really the custom,' Waleed said, 'for a widow to live with her in-laws. It's as if you're giving the signal to everyone that you don't want to get married again.'

'It doesn't matter . . . I don't really care what signal people get.'

He looked sad all of a sudden and when he spoke his voice was softer, childlike, her baby brother of long ago. 'I'm sorry, Sammar. I'm sorry that I'm your only family left and I can't take you and Amir in . . .'

The thought of her and Amir living with Waleed and his wife in their new flat was ridiculous enough to make her want to laugh out loud. But she controlled herself and in the silence caught some of Waleed's change of mood. His words 'I'm your only family left', and an awareness of their long-dead parents, a longing for them and what they could have offered.

'I've been sitting here,' she finally said to tease him, 'thinking you want to get rid of me and send me back to Aberdeen. Instead you want me and Amir right here with you, so that your wife will go mad and return to her father's house.'

He frowned and became his own irritated self, 'Of course you have to go back to your job in Aberdeen . . .'

She tousled his hair and gave him a hug. The neon light above their head buzzed, glowed and came on. Some of the streetlights blinked. 'Hey,' yelled the children and rushed indoors to the light of the sitting room.

The computer was on the dining table, swathed in plastic covers. The printer, similarly covered, was on the nearby sideboard. Sammar pulled out the dining chair that faced the monitor and sat down. The end of the power cut brought with it noisiness; the loud television, the purr of the air cooler, and from the bathroom she could hear the toilet filling up with water.

'So how do I get this computer to work?' she asked Waleed, who was telling the children that he didn't have any cartoon videos.

'I thought we agreed that you weren't going to resign.' He came over to her and frowned . . .

'No.'

'You're really hard-headed, you're not going to take my advice, are you?'

When she shook her head he shrugged and began to unveil his precious computer, lifting up the layers of plastic covers that protected it from dust. Everything was precious in Khartoum, even ink and paper, because it was all imported, so hard to replace.

It was not difficult to write the letter, she had handwritten it at home and just needed to type it then print it out. She needed two copies, the same wording but one addressed to Personnel, another to her head of Department. That was the normal procedure for resigning. She wrote 'family obligations' as the reason she could not leave Khartoum and come back to Aberdeen.

Waleed hovered around her as she wrote. 'I'll do the printing,' he said when she finished and shooed her out of the way.

The letters slid out of the printer, smoothly, one after the other. 'Isles,' said Waleed as he lifted the second letter, 'Professor R. Isles, an unusual name.'

'Yes, he's the head of department.' For months, weeks she had not said his name, not once. Not heard it once, nor said it once, even in a whisper, to herself. Now to Waleed she said, her voice too bright, 'Guess what the R stands for.'

'Richard?'

'No.'

'Ronald Reagan?'

'Don't be silly.'

'I give up,' he said, dusting the computer screen with a cloth that he took out of a plastic pouch. 'I'm not dying to know.'

'Rae,' she mumbled, mispronouncing his name. She wiped her hand on her skirt.

'Rye, *rai'* ?' said Waleed putting the cover back over the machine.

She smiled. *Rai'* was opinion in Arabic. 'Yes,' she said looking away. 'He had lots of opinions.'

18

S he sent the letters and told herself that she was not waiting, not expecting anything but an acknowledgement of her resignation, a formal response to her 'Dear Professor Isles . . .', something that one of the secretaries would type up for him, put a copy in his filing cabinet labelled 'Administration'.

In Khartoum, no postmen walked the streets, no letters were delivered to people's homes. Her aunt rented out a post-office box, owned a key that creaked opened a little metal door like a locker. Inside, the family's post would be found, lying on a film of dust. Sammar turned the key of the post-office box and found nothing.

In Egypt when she had spent day after day interpreting interviews in Cairo, Alexandria and the south, she had waited for a message from him, some word. He knew where she was, he knew how to get in touch with her. She needed him to say, I didn't mean it when I said get away from me, I didn't mean it. That was what she wanted in those tense days. Different hotels, everyone she was working with enjoying the location, appreciative of Egypt, going out to see all the sights, and she sick inside, not sure of anything except that she must work, work hard, stay numb, not cry. Three weeks' comforting herself, tomorrow he will get in touch with me, he knows where I am, tomorrow. She worked, she ate, she stayed in the same hotel with people who came from the same world he came from, worked in the same field. His competitors who wrote for the same journals he wrote for, went to the same conferences but in her eyes they were different than him, indistinct and cheerful compared to him. He could have been here, one of them, part of this programme. 'They took someone else,' he had said to her in the Winter Gardens, 'someone with more palatable views.' She had not understood what he meant by more palatable views.

He will get in touch with me, he will not leave me like this, she thought in Alexandria and in the southern province of Souhaig, and she thought wrong. She hoped and she worked hard pushing Arabic into English, English into Arabic, staying up late with hotel smells, typing out all the interviews. She looked as weary as the young men she put the questions to everyday, thin and disillusioned, their fingers gripping cigarettes, bravado and dreams. She put to them questions made up by others, then turned their answers into English words . . . 'I worked as a helper in a beauty salon, the usual things, sweeping hair from off the floor, washing towels . . .' 'My brother served time and when he came out . . .', 'My father worked in Baghdad and lost his job when the war broke out . . .', 'We live ten, one room . . .' When they spoke they addressed her. Only one of them looked her straight in the eye, baiting, different than the others, 'I was in America,' he said, 'Massachussetts. I was there so I know what I'm talking about. Western men worship money and women. Some of them see the world through dollar bills, some of them see the world through the thighs of a woman.' He spoke like that but she remained numb, numb about everything, silent when the others later, over lunch, could speak of nothing else. She smiled stupidly when she was told, 'I'm sorry you had to go through that. Most unpleasant.' She remained numb until she reached Khartoum, walked into her aunt's house and saw Tarig's picture on the wall.

*   *   *

She turned the key of the post-office box and found a reply from the Personnel Department. She owed the University one month's salary because she had not served her notice. She turned the key of the post-office box and found nothing, not even the formal reply she expected from him. She turned the key of the post-office box and found a letter from Yasmin. She had given birth to a baby girl, she was on maternity leave now, no longer going to work. There was no mention of Rae in the letter. There was the excitement of the baby and 'You are doing the right thing, Sammar, staying with your family, not coming back . . . we too would like to leave Britain . . .'

She turned the key of the post-office box and found nothing. She turned the key of the post-office box and knew she would find nothing. She gave the key back to Hanan, saying, 'I'm not expecting any more mail.' Even if he wrote what she wanted him to write, 'I didn't mean it when I said, get away from me', what would be the use? They could not have a future together, it would not be enough.

Her future was here where she belonged. She belonged with her son and strangers who smiled when she came into a room. She should not delude herself and with time she would forget. The sun and dust would erode her feelings for him. She must give away the bottle of perfume he had given her. She must pull his words out of her head like seaweed and throw them away.

Here. Her life was here.

Starting a new job, getting used to teaching, linking faces to names. Picking Amir and Dalia up from school. Housework, in the evening a social life, everyone indoors by the eleven o'clock curfew. Visitors or calling on people to offer condolences when death came, congratulations when a baby came. Welcome to the one who arrived from abroad, goodbye to the one who was going away. And bed-ridden people who spoke in faint voices, the smell of sick rooms.

Here. Her life was here.

Life was the dust storms that approached rosy brown from the sky, the rush to slam shut windows and doors, the wind whistling through bushes and trees. Brief mad storms and then the sand, thick sand covering everything, whirls of soft sand on the tiles to scoop up and throw away. To beat out of curtains, cushions, pillows, to dust away from the surface of all that was still. Sand eternally between the grooves of things, in folds of skin, the leaves of the children's books. And life was the rain that came at dawn with lightening, fat drops on the dust, the sun defeated for a day. Just a day, a softening, a picture of the past, the empty square covered in silver, laid out with the colour of the moon. Someone to talk to . . .

Remember Hanan, one day you and I walking in our school uniforms to get milk from the store. There was no school because of the rain. We went in the morning, found it closed and came back. But we stayed with our uniforms on all day.

Remember Sammar, how Tarig used to ride his bicycle through the puddles on purpose, every puddle from here to Airport Road.

Remember Hanan, the day we went to the Blue Nile cinema and it started to rain on top of our heads and Tarig just sat there watching the screen.

Remember the day, remember the time. Remember Tarig. Hassan looked like him, his uncle who had never seen him. Only Hassan not Hussein, they were not identical twins. Even Amir did not look like his father as much as Hassan did. Isn't that strange? she said to Hanan, as they folded the washing together, so much washing, hills of clean clothes to sort out and smooth into neat piles.

Week after week. Stroking Hassan's hair, watering the garden, removing seeds from slices of watermelon. Watching Hanan's baby grow, the first day he ate beans, the first day he tasted mangoes and how his nappy looked after that. The door bell and rushing from indoors, down the steps of the porch to drag open the black metal gate. Miranda for guests, ice cubes, a dish of sweets to pass around. 'Water,' some would say. 'Just get me a glass of water, Sammar, nothing else.' She fell in love with Amir again. She carried him around the house, like Hanan carried her baby. They played a game, they pretended Amir was a baby again and she had to carry him. Only in this game could he be sweet and clinging. At all other times, he was aloof, independent, never afraid. He neither remembered nor missed his father. He had lived quite content without his mother. There was something unendearing about her son: a strength, an inner privacy she knew nothing about, shut out by guilt and her years away. Only in this game of baby and mother were they close. Carrying him around the house, not minding that he was heavy. Do you know, baby, that you were born in a cold country and you wore white wool. Baby, do you want to go outside to the garden? Look, this is a tree, this is the grass. What's that? in his pretend baby voice, pointing up. What's that? An airplane. It takes people away, far away from here.

The new job. Different people, classes held in different locations. Some of the 'Erasing Illiteracy' classes were in the evening at the university. Palm trees and a campus shabby with crumbling walls, undergraduate students not so well dressed or healthy looking as the ones she used to see in Aberdeen. Like all the other evening classes, her class took a break for the sunset prayers. They would leave the room where the fan whirled overhead blowing sheets of paper off the desks, and step into the heat of outside. She never knew who spread out the palm-fibre mats on the grass. They were always there when she came out. Beige and a little rough on the forehead and the palms. When she stood her shoulders brushed against the women at each side of her, straight lines, then bending down together but not precisely at the same time, not slick, not synchronised, but rippled and the rustle of clothes until their foreheads rested on the mats. Under the sky, the grass underneath, it was a different feeling from praying indoors, a different glow. She remembered having to hide in Aberdeen, being alone. She remembered wanting him to pray like she prayed, hoping for it. The memory made her say, *Lord, keep sadness away from me.*

She kept busy so that there would not be pauses in the day to dwell. She tired herself so that there would not be dreams at night. Toilet training the twins, watching videos with everyone: thrilling American films, loud Egyptian soaps. Taking her aunt to the doctor, listening to her aunt on the way back, 'My son would have been a great doctor like him . . .'

Listening to Nahla for hours at a time, Nahla angry because her wedding must be indefinitely postponed, the reasons – a catalogue of problems – her fiancé's work, his lack of work, his frustrated desire to get a job abroad, the fact that they had nowhere to live, the fact that his father was loaded and yet too mean to help out.

She was rarely alone. Almost never alone. At night her aunt would turn over, sit up, pour herself a glass of water from the thermos she kept under her bed. Amir would mumble in his sleep, kick off the covers, dream children's dreams. First thing in the morning, Dalia would come down, trailing ribbons and comb, a smudged tube of Wellaform. 'Braid my hair, hurry, I'll be late for school.'

The Wellaform made Dalia's hair gleam and stuck on Sammar's fingers. She wiped them on her own hair and covered it before Dalia's father came down to bid his mother-in-law good morning, on his way to work. He worked in his family's ice factory. Every morning he said the same thing, 'Do you need anything?' and every morning her aunt replied, 'Only your well-being.' Though at any other time of the day she would want him to do this and that, bring this and that, sending messages through Hanan. Sometimes, if there was time, he had coffee with her aunt, Sammar stirring the sugar, offering biscuits. Most often the morning was a rush and he did not have time to sit down. He would hold Dalia by the hand, pretty in her school uniform and braids, greet his mother-in-law and say, 'Do you need anything, Aunt?'

What was life like? Deprivation and abundance, side by side like a miracle. Surrender to them both. Poverty and sunshine, poverty and jewels in the sky. Drought and the gushing Nile. Disease and clean hearts. Stories from neighbours, relations.

A twenty-year-old smitten with polio, look at him now overweight and ungainly, walking with a crutch.

On the operating table, before they knocked me out with the anaesthetic, I saw flies buzzing above my head . . .

No this and no that. No water. In this land where the Nile flooded, no water. No water to have a shower with, flush the toilets with, cook, drink. Driving in the car across town to fill big Jerry cans with water from someone else's garden tap. Tipping buckets of water down the toilet, scooping water from a pail to bathe.

Tempers were short during a water cut. Even shorter than during a power cut. When the water came back, it spluttered and spat out of the taps, dark brown with sediment, poisonous black. Gradually it would lighten. Even then they had to filter it before they drank it or cooked with it. A challenge just to live from day to day, a struggle just to get by. But there were jokes. Jokes about the cuts, rationing and the government. Laughter on hot evenings in the garden, her aunt smiling like in the past, grasshoppers and frogs as loud as the children.

And everyday Amir in his school uniform, white shirt streaked with sweat and dust, scruffy shoes. 'Why did you lose your pencil?' . . . 'No, you're not allowed to buy candy floss from the man at the gate. It's full of germs.'

This was her life. Fighting malaria, penicillin powder on the children's cuts. The curfew at eleven. Immersing herself, losing herself so that there would not be pauses in the day to dwell, no time for fantasies at night.

19

But she dreamt of him. Dreams in which he brushed past her, would not look at her, would not speak to her. Dreams in which he was busy talking to others. When she sought his attention he frowned and it was a cold look that she received, no fondness. She would wake after such dreams with raw eyes, mumbling and clumsy, dropping things, mislaying things. When asked what was wrong with her, she would say that it was the time of month.

No news of him, his name. In Yasmin's letters, the words slanting and large: her baby daughter doesn't sleep through the night, her baby is teething, a photo of the baby, no mention of Rae. When she answered Yasmin's letters she disciplined herself not to ask about him, not to ask for news or even a casual reference like the remarks she used to hear in Aberdeen all around her in abundance, from Diane, from the coffee-scented secretaries, from his Ph.D. students, the man from Sierra Leone. What she wanted to know: how was he, how was his health, did he have any new Ph.D. students, where did he publish the paper he and Fareed were working on, who translated for him now? This she asked Yasmin, this she finally allowed herself but without using his name, without writing it down. 'Did they find anyone to take my place?' she wrote. But Yasmin was on extended maternity leave, in another world with her baby girl, not keen to go back to work, not very interested. She wrote, 'No, I don't think the department has anyone translating for them at the moment, I'm not sure.' And Sammar found herself nostalgic for her old job, the work itself, moulding Arabic into English, trying to be transparent like a pane of glass not obscuring the meaning of any word. She missed the cramped room with the hum of the computer. She missed Diane, the smell of her cheese and onion crisps, her innocence when she said, 'Rae's class was really good today. One bloke asked this question about . . .'

This was the exile from him then. Never hearing his name. Living in a place where no one knew him. And when weak from the dreams, needing to speak of him and not being able to. She wanted to say anything, however meaningless. At times with a friend, Nahla, even with Hanan, she would want to speak about him. A question from them would be the trigger, a question about her time in Scotland. A question followed by a pause in the conversation, the possibility of a turning point and then other words would fill up the space. She was afraid of the sound of her voice talking about him, the silliness of it and feeling ashamed. She knew that they would stop at him being a foreigner, their mind would close after that. Wide eyes, surprise, a *foreigner*? They would imagine him like someone in an American film. The kind of videos they watched: a bodyguard, a man who was really a robot with skin. She did not want them to imagine him like that. Their eyes rimmed with kohl, warm, wide, and she knowing what was in their minds, having to somehow defend him, stammer through the questions they would ask.

'No, he's different, not really . . .'

'Half-foreign?'

'No, he's just different, not . . . impatient, not . . . cool.'

'I still can't believe it. A *Christian*?'

'Not really, no.'

'What do you mean?'

'He's not religious, he doesn't go to church. He's not sure . . .'

'Not *sure*?'

'He believes in Allah but when I asked him if he accepts that Muhammad, peace be upon him is a Messenger, he said he wasn't sure.'

'*You*, Sammar, of all people? You're not like modern girls who marry foreigners. You're not the type.'

'Anyway it didn't work. It failed.'

'But *why* did you let yourself get involved in the first place?'

Start to talk of him and she would have to answer all sorts of questions, become hot with shyness and what she couldn't say, that she had tipped over, begged him: just say the *shahadah*, just say the words and it would be enough, we could get married then. It was not a story to be proud of. Perhaps Hanan would repeat it to her husband, something to amuse him after a hard day's work. Perhaps Nahla would repeat it to her mother, a piece of gossip from next door. It was sensible to keep quiet, keep busy, forget. She talked to herself, she told herself that she did not know him. She did not understand the words 'sixties' scene' or a Saturday afternoon in Edinburgh when he got married in a church and wore a kilt. How could she understand things like that, be connected to them? She gave herself lectures when the dreams came and weakened her. 'I must start a new life, stop being sentimental, stop feeling sorry for myself. Everyone around me is deprived of something or another. Some people don't even have running water in their homes. And all the babies that die and inflation tight around people's throats. I am so lucky I can afford medicine for my son and Eid clothes, decent meals, even luxuries, useless things like renting videos. I should be thankful. If I was good, if my faith was strong, I would be grateful for what I have.'

But she still dreamt of him. Vivid dreams in which he brushed past her, close, close enough for her to smell him but he would not look at her, would not talk to her. In one dream she was as short as a child in a room full of adults and smoke. She was in this room to look for him and she was standing near a table that was large and high. On tiptoe she saw that the table was green, a solid rectangular green with no cutlery, no food or drinks. She reached with her hand and it was as if the table was a shallow box lined with green rough wool. On the other side of the table Rae was talking to a man she did not recognise, a man with glasses and straight black hair sliding over his eyes. The room was choked with people bigger than her, older than her. Their discontent buzzed through the room, through the smoke, and, like in the other dreams, Rae came towards her and then brushed past her, distracted, unaware of her because she was too young and too short for him.

Raw eyes in the morning, the way a dream affects the day ahead. The ceiling fan rotated slowly distributing the breeze that came from the window. The birds were strident outside. The way a dream threatens the day, sharpens a memory. Only a dream and it could induce nausea in her, a dry soreness behind her eyes.

She poured sour milk in her aunt's tea and had to make another cup. She sent Amir to school without making him brush his teeth, left the fan running in the empty bedroom all morning. At work she felt that she didn't care, it didn't matter at all that her adult students could barely read and write. The illiteracy rate was 60 or 82 per cent depending on who was right, and today she had no energy or desire to reduce it.

'What's wrong with you? Are you tired?' she was asked. 'Sister, please raise your voice we can't hear you.' It was women's classes in the morning: mothers, grandmothers, today instead of reading, a health lesson about breastfeeding. The reading syllabus was set by a government commission and because of the shortage of books, children's school books were used. The same books from which Dalia and Amir were taught. *I am a girl. I come from the village. I am a boy. I come from the village. This is a camel. These are dates.* It was humiliating to learn from such books. She could feel it in their voices, a kind of edge, the men (who made up the majority in the evening classes) more so than the women, who would laugh it off, saying, 'Now I can read my children's school books.' For this reason health topics and community education lessons were more successful. It was lucky for her that on the day she was least motivated, the topic was the popular one of feeding babies.

'You left the fan on in the bedroom all morning,' said her aunt, the now familiar contempt in her eyes, her voice a certain way, wanting war. They were her first words when Sammar, Amir and Dalia came home. Dalia sucking a lollipop given to her by a friend, Amir trailing his school bag, pretending not to be envious. Sammar took off her sunglasses, poured herself a glass of water from the fridge. She sat on one of the children's stools in front of the blowing air cooler, put her glass of water on the coffee table. There was condensation on the glass because the water was cold.

'I'm sorry,' she said. She could not say that it was because of the dream. Everything going wrong because of the dream. She started to drink her glass of water. Nile water beautiful after thirst, *alhamdulillah.*

'Electricity isn't free,' said Mahasen. She was sitting on one of the beds putting Hanan's baby to sleep, patting him on the back as he lay on his side facing the wall. Hanan was still at work. She worked longer hours than Sammar, she was more productive, more efficient. The baby raised his head up and smiled at Sammar. She smiled back, mouthed his name silently. Mahasen patted him harder. 'Come on, sleep!' she said to him.

Sammar felt that her aunt wanted to say more, that there was more to come after the statement 'Electricity isn't free.' She escaped, went to the bedroom to change, then called Amir to give him a shower so that he could be clean before he ate. He talked to her while she towelled and dressed him but she was not listening, her mind numb behind her dry eyes, the fear that she was somehow not going to able to complete the day, that it was too long, too much of a challenge. Even when she prayed she still felt a tightness inside, a sense of foreboding.

The main meal of the day served as usual and Hanan's twins were brought down by their father, who went upstairs again. The children sat on the stools around the table. The clutter of plastic dishes, murmurs from her, 'Say *bismillah* before you eat. Be good and finish your plate.' They were sometimes lively, sometimes quiet. Today after the first few mouthfuls it was as if devils danced around the house, skipped on top of the furniture, goaded the children. Rice scattered everywhere, there were screeches, fights, rice grains in noses and ears. Amir pinched Dalia, stuck his tongue out at her. Dalia bit Amir, leaving saliva, chewed rice and ridges on his arm. He pulled her hair, yanked it and she screamed, a scream so loud that it seemed incredible to Sammar, as she pulled them apart, that such a noise could come out of someone Dalia's size. Devils danced around the room making everything a blur in front of Sammar's eyes. Millions of children babbling away, the rattle and the din of plastic plates and she in the middle of it, immersed, hypnotised. Dalia's scream woke the baby, his arms grasped the air, his face scrunched with anger, his own kind of screaming. Mahasen picked him up and started to rock him in her arms. If he did not have a proper nap, he was grumpy the rest of the day.

'Make them quiet,' Mahasen shouted. 'Do something, Sammar, instead of staring at them like an idiot.'

But the children were wild, stronger than her. They rotated around the room, shouting, kicking. They ran too fast. At last Hanan appeared at the door like a hero, solid and in control, dignified in her dentist's working clothes. She smacked Dalia, picked up her screaming baby and herded her messy twins upstairs. She left Sammar with Dalia whimpering and clinging, and a dull calmness all around the room. As if nothing had happened, Amir arranged his toy cars on the floor, talked to them and pushed them carefully from the carpet to the tiles.

'All this is because you are useless,' said her aunt. 'A few children and you don't know how to handle them. I don't know what happened to you. In the past you were lively and strong, now you've just become an idiot.'

She wanted to escape from her aunt but Dalia was clinging to her, sticky and limp. She wanted to escape into cleaning the room, sweeping up the rice that was scattered on the table and on the floor.

'You don't even have a proper job, a job that pays. How much have you been contributing to the house?'

'Not much,' her voice flat, obedient, answering how Mahasen wanted her to answer.

'And content to wear others' clothes, without *any* pride.'

That was true. She had been passed on a whole wardrobe of Hanan's, clothes that were too tight for her after having the baby, didn't fit anymore. And it was also true, that she had no pride. The clothes, when Hanan offered them, had made her happy. They were loose on her, long. Hanan had been nice, she had said, as Sammar tried each thing on, looking at herself in the full length mirror, turning this way and that, 'Everything looks lovely on you, Sammar.' Now her aunt was making it all dirty, wanting her to feel ashamed.

'You should go back to England, work there and send us things.'

'I don't want to go back.'

'We buried the deceased and you went around saying, "It's a good thing he left me with one child, not three or four, what would I have done with them?" A thing to say. It shows how low you are, with no manners, no respect for his memory. Now you have this one child and you don't even want to take him to England and look out for his benefit.'

She wanted to wash the dishes, smell soap, the soothing fall of the water on spoons and plates, but she was pinned down by Dalia, her little sobs, her head on her lap. Someone must have repeated her words to Mahasen. She had never told Mahasen that she was glad she had only one child. And now all this could lead to the old quarrel about 'Am Ahmed, bringing that up all over again . . .

'I know what happened,' her aunt went on, her voice and the steady roar of the air cooler. 'I know why you came back. They fired you, didn't they, because you didn't do the work well? Don't think I'm fooled by this story of you going to Waleed and sending off a resignation letter or the rubbish you said about being homesick for your country. Foreigners don't stand for nonsense, I know. Their countries wouldn't be so advanced if they did,' she gestured vaguely at the unlit screen of the television, her source of knowledge about the world. 'You were just no good and they told you to leave.'

'No.' She stared down at Dalia's head on her lap, her hair sticking out of the braids.

'You're a liar.'

'I'm not a liar.' She smoothed Dalia's hair, her hands cold, clumsy.

'You're a liar and you killed my son.'

She shook her head, not sure if her aunt meant what she said and it was not her muddled mind that was imagining it all. It was not a line from an Egyptian soap that her aunt was repeating. 'You killed my son,' Mahasen had actually spoken those words out loud. Now on her face there was a kind of triumph as if she had finally, from deep inside, pulled out what she had always wanted to say.

The denial stuck in Sammar's throat.

'You nagged him to buy that car,' her aunt's words were focused now, distinct. 'You nagged him day and night and he sent for money.'

Sammar shook her head. She hadn't known, she hadn't known

that he was short of money, that he had asked his mother. 'He didn't tell me,' she said breathing through the fear, the fear that her mind *would* bend, surrender to this madness, accept the accusation, live forever with the guilt.

'You nagged him for that car and that car killed him. He wrote and said, "Please, Mama, help me, Sammar's getting on my nerves, saying it's cold, it's too cold to walk everywhere, let's get a car." Then I sent him the money.'

Tarig wrote to Mahasen, complaining . . . Sammar's getting on my nerves . . . It sounded so much like him, the way he would speak, Sammar's getting on my nerves. It jumped up at her in spite of the years, in spite of the gulf between their world and his. It sounded so much like him, the way he would speak. The way he spoke to his mother sometimes, as if there was some kind of conspiracy against him, threatening his career. He had been like that . . . Sammar tried to remember the time before they bought the car, she tried to remember nagging him. It was years ago. He hadn't told her he was short of money, he hadn't told her that he had written to Mahasen asking for money. She had thought he wanted a car as much as she did. And now he was not here for her to ask him. Her aunt's words hung in the air, a banner of victory, they could not be contradicted or denied.

'Dalia, get up,' she eased the child's head away from her lap. Dalia sat up and rubbed her eyes. Sammar began to clear the plates off the table and to sweep the rice off the floor. She could feel her aunt watching how inefficient she was, clumsy in her movements, slow. She felt cold, her bones cold and stiff, not moving smoothly, not moving with ease. She wanted a bed and a cover, sleep. She wanted to sleep like she used to sleep in Aberdeen, everything muffled up and grey, curling up, covering her face with the blanket, her breath warming the cocoon she had made for herself.

Amir pushed a tape into the video and cheerful music filled the room. Dalia sat cross-legged on the floor and watched Mary

Poppins flying in the air. Mahasen lay down on the bed, propped up on her elbow watching the television. There was a peaceful expression on her face, as if she was drained now, fulfilled after her outburst.

Sammar's fingers were steady as she washed the dishes. The water spluttered and gushed out of the tap. There were colours in the soap suds, pink, green. She rinsed the glasses and stood them face down to dry, moved her weight from one foot to another. Something to lean on, rest upon, be held up by. If she could believe that he loved her, that now he was aware of her . . . But she didn't believe, could not make herself believe. It was not there inside her. Inside her was only a bright hardness. Months since she had seen him, months since she had left Aberdeen. He was far away. He had forgotten her, he was a foreigner and she was who she was. By now he must know another woman. It was so long since he had lived with his wife, one had to be realistic about these things. His world had different rules. Perhaps he was relieved when she left, all the messiness of it, the sticky complications. Another woman, more easily accessible, lighter. A woman with lighter eyes, a lighter heart, someone who didn't care whether he believed in God or not.

When she finished washing the dishes, Sammar went and stood at the door to the sitting room. She watched Dalia squint a little in front of the television. Mahasen was sitting up on the bed rubbing cream on her hand and flexing her fingers to ease the joints. She wanted to say to her aunt that no one killed Tarig, it just happened, it was his day. She wanted to say that Allah gives life and takes it, and she had no feeling of guilt for wanting Tarig to buy a car. She was not to blame. If he had told her he was short of money, she would have understood and accepted. But he hadn't told her. She wanted to say to her aunt, be careful when you speak of the dead because they are not here to defend themselves. Why tell me that he had complained about me, that he said I got on his nerves? He would not have wanted me to know this.

Mahasen looked up, 'Did you finish?'

'Yes.'

Mahasen looked down at her hands again, smoothed the white cream over her loose skin.

It was time for Sammar to talk now, say what she wanted to say.

'When I say you should go back to England,' said Mahasen, 'it is for your own good and Amir's. Not for my own good. Amir fills the house and you serve me . . .'

The house. Of course there must be a mention of the house. They shared ownership of this house . . .

'It is better for us to be here,' Sammar said. What she had intended to say when she came out of the kitchen effervesced. Her voice was sullen as a child, 'I didn't lose my job, they didn't dismiss me, I left of my own accord.'

Mahasen sighed as if she did not believe her, as if she was humouring her. 'Yes, alright,' she said and turned to look at the television again.

The bedroom was not so hot. It was bearable with the ceiling fan and the shutters closed against the sun. The room smelt of her aunt, a smell of creams and cologne. Sammar sat up on the bed, leaned against the wall, hugged her knees and stared at the cracks on the ceiling. Some were angry and painful, some were delicate and faint: a European woman from long ago in a billowing dress, a cedar tree. She wished she could feel that Rae was close to her in spite of the angry words she had said to him, in spite of his get away, get away from me. She prayed that she could feel him close, not like in the dream, not distracted, not brushing past her. If she would dream a good dream about him. One good dream, reassuring her. He was so far away now that she could not imagine his voice, could not believe the things he had said to her. Another exile. Doubt, the exile of not being sure that anything existed between them, no tangible proof. The perfume he had given was in another room locked in a suitcase with all that she didn't need: wool and tights, her duffle coat. All the clothes he had seen her in, locked away in the storeroom with sacks of lentils and rice.

She was weak today. Because of last night's dream and she had annoyed her aunt. She couldn't remember clearly what she had done to annoy her aunt, to trigger all that came out of her. The cracks on the ceiling. The fan? The children? The children running around like devils, making a terrible noise, then after Hanan came and went, her aunt said things . . . Her aunt blamed her for Tarig's death. That was bizarre. She wished that Hanan had been present or Waleed then she would have felt sane and safe, maybe not so frightened. They would have defended her. Even if they were silent out of respect for her aunt, she would have felt that they were on her side. Rae was on her side. He had told her that in the hospital when she showed him her aunt's letter, the address on the envelope, Aberdeen, England. He said, you've won me to your side in any quarrel you have with your aunt. That was what he had said. She could remember it now. She could remember. The hospital and how the glass door of the entrance was difficult to push. The way he looked when he saw her. She could remember now. Smile, gaze up at the lady in the hooped skirt and the branches of the cedar tree.

It was a joke. You've won me to your side, Sammar, in any quarrel you have with your aunt. It was a joke about the address and she had laughed. Someone in the post office had crossed out England with red ink. She had shown him the envelope and he had held it in his hand. There was a plaster at the back of his hand from the intravenous amoxilyn. He had thought she looked nice. She was wearing her new coat, henna-coloured and toggles instead of buttons. It was warm in the ward, too warm, and she had wanted to take the coat off but she had felt too shy. When he told her he loved her it was strange because no one had told her these words in English before. And it was not like in a film, it was just like the way he spoke, normal. If now she could have anything she wanted, she would want to look at photographs of him when he was young, black and white photographs and early coloured ones. His hair and the clothes he wore. She would like to look at his photographs and ask him questions. He would be more interested in her than in the photographs, answering her questions reluctantly, not so keen as she was to talk about the past. It was because of the way he looked at her that things came to a head, the awkwardness she felt, uneasy with everything. If they were not a man and a woman, if they were pure friends, if all that was between them was clear air, she would have been patient when she asked him if he believed and he replied, 'I am not sure.'

There were people who drew others to Islam. People with deep faith, the type who slept little at night, had an energy in them. They did it for no personal gain, no worldly reason. They did it for Allah's sake. She had heard stories of people changing: prisoners in Brixton, a German diplomat, an American with ancestors from Greece. Someone influencing someone, with no ego involved. And she, when she spoke to Rae, wanting this and that, full of it; wanting to drive with him to Stirling, to cook for him, to be settled, to be someone's wife.

She had never, not once, prayed that he would become a Muslim for his own sake, for his own good. It had always been for herself, her need to get married again, not be alone. If she could rise above that, if she would clean her intentions. He had been kind to her and she had given him nothing in return. She would do it now from far away without him ever knowing. It would be her secret. If it took ten months or ten years or twenty or more.

20

'This is my first Ramadan since I came back,' she said, in answer to Waleed's question.

'Yes, you weren't with us last year,' said Mahasen as she reached for another piece of bread. Sammar had cut the loaves into small portions. Such thin loaves these days, shrinking while their price threatened to go up.

The three of them were eating in the garden. No electric lights competed with the moon, no garden lights. The candle Sammar had brought from inside was unnecessary and she blew it out.

It was the middle of the month of Ramadan and the moon was full. From tomorrow it would shrink and lose itself. When the new crescent appeared it would be the end of Ramadan. The end of fasting, visitors saying Eid Mubarak and new clothes for the children.

It was unusual to be alone with Waleed and Mahasen, without anyone else, without the children. Hanan and her family were with their in-laws and they had taken Amir with them. It was supposed to be only Sammar and Mahasen breaking the fast together but at the first words of the sunset azan, before they had time to eat any dates, the door bell rang. When Sammar dragged open the garden gate, it was Waleed. She had been so pleased to see him and surprised, that she hugged him and he said, 'What's the matter with you?'

'What's the matter with you coming alone without your wife?'

'She's eating with her parents,' he said and nothing more. Sammar didn't ask him why he had not gone too, it became busy with the three of them breaking their fast, dates and *kerkedeh,* her aunt saying to Waleed, 'If we knew you were coming we would have made grapefruit juice.'

After Sammar put the jug of *kerkedeh* back in the fridge and threw away the date stones, they prayed. They prayed together with Waleed leading and Sammar and Mahasen standing close, their arms and clothes touching. Mahasen's movements were slow when she bent down, knelt down and put her forehead on the mat. Sammar felt Waleed deliberately pausing, slowing his pace so that Mahasen could keep up. When they finished praying there was a power cut. The sudden silence of the air cooler, the sudden loss of the lights, the fan slowing down. In the stillness and faint glow of sunset, Sammar counted on her fingers twenty-seven times, *There is no god but Allah and I seek forgiveness from Allah for my wrongs and for believing men and believing women . . .*

Her aunt's voice was loud in the room, 'Allah curse them and their day, is this a time for this?' 'Them' was the electricity company and the government, the two inseparable to Mahasen. She went on, 'They've made us hate life . . .' The room without the air cooler was gradually getting warm but they could still see each other without the lights.

Waleed stood up and folded his prayer mat. 'Aunt, the supplication of the one who is fasting is granted,' he smiled. 'The electricity company must be in a bad way by now.'

'The whole neighborhood is cursing them,' said Mahasen standing up.

Sammar took the mat from Waleed and picked up hers and her aunt's off the floor. It seemed to her funny if the whole neighborhood was really cursing the company, all that energy rising up in the sunset air. Some people were so serious about power cuts. Like her aunt, getting angry to the core.

'Let's eat outside in the garden, Aunt,' she said and Mahasen sighed and nodded in agreement. Since that bad day when Mahasen had said, 'You killed my son,' the relationship between them had strangely improved, mellowed. It was as if Mahasen had said the worst she could possibly say and there were no more accusations after that.

In the kitchen, by candlelight, Sammar heated the food, her shadow swinging huge against the walls. The kitchen was hot and airless without the fan and she could hear the cockroaches stir and dart across the floor. But once they were seated outside, cushions on the chairs, a tablecloth on the wobbly table and there was a breeze, the food tasted good and it felt better than indoors. Much better than a normal day eating indoors with the air cooler and all the lights.

'Last Ramadan,' said Mahasen, scooping up stew with her piece of bread, 'not once did the electricity cut. Things are supposed to get better and they just get worse.'

Waleed did not speak much when he was eating. Grunts of agreement with his aunt and, 'Pour me water, Sammar.' He looked tired, she thought, not just the normal tiredness from fasting. He might have quarrelled with his wife and that was why he had not gone with her to her parents. Instead he was here with them today and Mahasen was being tactful, not asking questions, glad to see him. Mahasen could be surprisingly tactful when it suited her. Waleed's presence livened her up. If it had been only her and Sammar, she would have been silent and withdrawn.

When they finished eating, Sammar carried the dishes to the kitchen and made tea. She put mint leaves in the pot, topped the sugar bowl with sugar. She put the candle on the tray to make her way back outside, walked from the kitchen to the hall to the sitting room, holding the tray with one hand and opening the door to the porch with another, closing it behind her so that stray cats would not creep in. On the porch there was the grey light of the moon on the pots of cactus plants and dark bougainvillea. She could blow out the candle now, walk down the steps of the porch to the voices of her aunt and Waleed.

The peace of sitting with them and not talking, not even listening while they talked. Waleed expansive now after the meal and with a glass of tea in his hand, making Mahasen smile. This good feeling was because of Ramadan, because of eating and drinking after fasting all day when the sun was too hot and it was thirst more than hunger, and not wanting to speak to anyone, economising words, saying what was only necessary, what was only enough to get by. A whole month free like that and looking up at the round moon, knowing that the month was half way through, two weeks and the focus would be gone. The closeness to the depth would be gone.

Tonight, like last night and every night until the end of Ramadan, she would wake up hours before dawn, pray once and again, read the Qur'an. This was the time of night when prayers were answered, this was the time of year . . .

'Sammar, isn't Nahla's fiancé working for Abu Dhabi's electricity company?' asked her aunt.

'Qatar, not Abu Dhabi. He's in Doha now.'

'So he managed to get a good job after all.' There was admiration in Waleed's voice, envy under control.

'Yes, after fuss and quarrels and they had to postpone the wedding twice,' said Mahasen. 'That girl was supposed to get married months ago and now she's still sitting.'

'Working for Qatar's national electricity company is a very good job,' said Waleed. 'How did he get it?'

'Someone who knew someone,' said Sammar.

'Of course someone knew someone,' he said, not unkindly, 'but who?'

'I don't know. I could find out for you.'

'I was just asking,' he said dismissively and finished his glass of tea.

'They're not going to get married until December,' said Sammar addressing her aunt. 'Nahla told me yesterday. They have the visa to sort out and she has re-sits. She wants to graduate before she goes there.'

'That's better for her. Qatar is good, she can get a good job there.' Mahasen said vehemently. She wanted everyone to get wonderful jobs, make good money, rise up in the world.

'I have a friend in Qatar,' said Sammar, 'a Pakistani woman I knew in Aberdeen. Her husband works in oil and he got transferred there. She likes it very much.' Yasmin was in Doha now, with her daughter and Nazim. Yasmin was not even in the same country as Rae anymore. Sammar could no longer write and ask her for news of him. When the option had been open to her, she hadn't, but now it still counted as a loss and she thought, 'I have no link with him now, in terms of people. Who do I know who knows him? Diane? Fareed? Neither of them can I ever have the courage to write to.'

But there were other links, a dream, an awareness that would suddenly come and stay with her. One day in the garden with the children, her feet bare and wearing another of Hanan's unwanted dresses, she had stood admiring the mud of the flower beds, under the jasmine bushes, the way it was smooth and dimpled. She had pressed her toe into the mud, made a little depression, and then she had knelt down and touched the mud with her fingers. It was like dough or plasticine and yet her fingers stayed clean when she looked at them. Clean, heavy mud. He was like that, heavy inside, not like other people. It was there with him when he came into a room and when he paused in the middle of saying something, paused before he answered a question she had asked.

Another time, opening the fridge to get her aunt a glass of water. The sudden chill when she opened the fridge door on a day that was too hot; the blue cold, frost and it was Aberdeen where he was, his jacket and walking in grey against the direction of the wind. White seagulls and a pale sea, until her aunt behind her shouted, 'What *are* you doing standing like an idiot with the door of the fridge wide open. Everything will melt.'

It was like that at first, the moment in the garden and the moment in front of the fridge, vivid, sudden. But the more she prayed for him, the more these moments came until they were there all the time, not only thoughts, not only memories but an awareness that stayed.

Waleed talked to her aunt and the moon was still unchallenged by the lights of the city below. Here was a gift for her, clearer than water, clearer than the sky . . .

Rae saying, 'I dreamt of you, the same dream. I am climbing stairs, steep stone steps, stairways that are damp and narrow. At the top I open a door and you are there.'

'Am I happy to see you?'

'You are . . . very much. You give me a glass of milk to drink.'

'*Milk*, how childish of me!'

'But when I drink it something happens. It can only happen in a dream . . . Pearls come out of my mouth, they fall in my hand. I hold them out and show them to you.'

21

December. A cool wind blowing, carrying dust, and everyone's skin was chapped. She thought, 'I love this time of year,' and looked out of the car window at the trees that lined Nile Avenue: thick trunks and behind them the gushing Blue Nile. She looked, she took off her sunglasses and looked until her heart hurt.

Nahla was driving. They had gone to the video shop and then Nahla had picked up her wedding cards from the printers. The cards were on Sammar's lap, stiff white envelopes in packets.

'Why are you quiet today?' asked Nahla.

'Just looking around. Do you think you will miss Khartoum when you go to Qatar?' At the end of December Nahla was going to get married and go away, move to Doha where Yasmin was, with her daughter and Nazim. If she ever could afford it, Sammar would go and visit them both.

'I don't know,' said Nahla. 'Not at first, maybe later. Now we just want to get away, we've been delayed so much.'

'Insha' Allah everything will go alright this time.'

'Sometimes I'm afraid,' said Nahla, changing gears, 'sometimes I think someone's going to die either from my family or his. Some senile uncle or grandmother or aunt is going to drop dead any minute and ruin everything.'

Sammar laughed. 'Just say insha' Allah something like that won't happen.' There was a boat on the river, its sails beige and brown, there were farmers on the opposite bank, bent over with hoes. The sun hit the moving water and made its surface light, but underneath it was blue after blue.

Last December in another place, there was no sun. Christmas, and Rae was in Edinburgh with his ex-wife's parents, presents wrapped up for Mhairi. Did he still do the same things? Drive around Scotland listening to Bob Marley, *Ambush in the night, all guns aiming at me* . . . Did he mark students' essays, watch CNN and VH-1, read lots of books. Sometimes say, 'I'm an old-fashioned socialist,' sometimes say, '. . . behind the Western propaganda of Islamic fundamentalism'. A year in his world might be shorter than in hers, not so many changes. Here new laws were passed, prices went up, the old died easy and children grew and changed. Did he still use the same Ventolin inhaler? Did he teach his students that the difference between Western liberalism and Islam was that the centre of one was freedom and the other justice? She didn't know what he was doing, this moment, this day but it didn't matter, he was near like in the dream. A dream of night on the porch, no moonlight and she was a child playing, square tiles, hopscotch. Many people were on the porch, adults standing talking in the dark and he was one of them. She saw him and it did not surprise her that he was here in this continent, in this country, on her aunt's porch. She was content to play, her hands on the wooden rails, skipping down the steps, the lines of the tiles. She lost sight of him and forgot him like children forget, her mind on the steps until he put his hand on her shoulder and when she looked up, he smiled and said, 'Did you think I wouldn't find you in the dark?' She did not say anything, she became perfect and smooth like water from the garden hose.

What kept her going day after day: he would become a Muslim before he died. It was not too much to want, not too much to pray for. They would meet in Paradise and nothing would go wrong there, nothing at all.

Yesterday she and Mahasen had gone to visit Tarig's grave. Driving out of the city to where there were no buildings blocking the wind. Travelling and finding flat ground, sand, knowing Tarig was there. Greeting him and all the others. Her aunt sat down on the ground, not moving, the Qur'an unopened on her lap. They found dirty things on the graves, things that the wind had carried through the barbed-wire fence. Orange peel, an empty cigarette carton, the remnant of a nest. A Miranda bottle top, indented and blurred. It grazed Sammar's hand when she picked it up. She started to clear the ground, on her hands and knees reaching out, careful, she must not step over the people lying underneath. 'We should get that keeper fired, *he* should be doing this,' she said to her aunt but got no answer. She was afraid of finding worse than the rubbish she was now collecting: the signs of stray dogs. The keeper's job was to keep stray dogs out, keep the cemetery clean, protect the graves from thieves. But he was not, thought Sammar, as a keeper of graves should be. He did not have clean white hair, a prayer mat, a melodious voice which recited the Qur'an. Instead he was young and gangly with broken teeth and a smell of hashish. Now as she gathered the rubbish, he stood leaning on the wall of his room, leering at her from far away. It made her angry and she went up to him and said, 'If I find dog-shit, you will have to start looking for another job.' He whined some excuse and skulked into the darkness of his room. She shouted after him, 'I am not joking, you know.' She felt safe with all the graves around her, all the truth. Cleaning up: a greasy newspaper page with the familiar face of a politician, a razor blade, some leaves. When she finished, she washed from the tap near the keeper's room, made *wudu* again. She sat next to her aunt, put her arms around her, kissed her cheek. Then she took from her the Qur'an and started to read, word after word, verse after verse, page after page.

*　　*　　*

'Come in for a while,' she said, when Nahla stopped the car in front of the house.

'No thanks, there's no time.'

'Come and show the cards to Aunt Mahasen.'

'I'll come in for a little while. But I might as well park the car at home.'

While Sammar waited in the street so that she and Nahla could go in together, she spoke to Rae. She told him about the poster she had seen in the video shop, an advertisement for an American film, the actors' names written in Arabic and English. She told him how the film's name was translated in Arabic. *'Look Who's Talking,'* she said, 'became in Arabic, *Me And Mama And Travolta'*. He laughed and said, 'That's a much better name'. He laughed and she saw Hanan driving round the corner, Amir in the front seat, Dalia in the back. When they saw Sammar waiting at the door, they started to wave.

She pushed open the black metal door for them so that Hanan could drive into the shade of the car-port. The door was heavy and it dragged on the ground, making grooves.

Hanan parked the car, switched the engine off. Amir and Dalia jumped out and the sounds of greetings was mixed up with the sound of slamming doors. 'There's a letter for you,' said Dalia and hope was a reflex, as silly as blinking.

Sammar reached for the envelope, the platinum face of the Queen, pearls around her neck. But she would know his handwriting. This was not his handwriting. She should not have hoped, this was not his handwriting.

Instead her name was written in Arabic, the envelope stamped in Stirling. Intrigue and the feel of paper tearing, the children's voices, Nahla greeting Hanan.

The signature first. Fareed. Fareed Khalifa? Why would he write to her? The memory of meeting him in Aberdeen, Rae introducing them. Questions, he asked a lot of questions, he used to be a journalist and he was imprisoned by the Israelis. 'They gave him a rough time,' Rae had said, 'they gave him a real rough time.' Skim the lines of polite greetings, search and Rae's name was there. At last after all the months of just wanting his name. Here it was, *I am writing to you on behalf of my friend Rae Isles.* Skim the lines down the page: . . . *became a . . . about four months ago . . . at my house . . . how pleased I am that Allah had expanded his heart to this . . . Ramadan . . . your permission . . . if you accept . . .*

Again, go over it again to catch every word, to really believe. The rush of this new knowledge, the feeling of being lifted up. She could even see herself, her head bent over the letter, her smile. Red flowers on her scarf falling on her shoulders. The navy cardigan, buttons undone, her folded sunglasses sticking out of the pocket. Her skirt touched the faded straps of her sandals, was creased at the back from sitting in the car. And the easy way she moved away from the children, away from Hanan and Nahla, away from the car-port to the garden. For she was being honoured now, she was being rewarded. All alone, a miracle for no one else to acknowledge but her. The sky had parted, a little crack, and something had pierced her life. Under the eucalyptus tree and the sound of the birds, kneel down . . . the clean Vicks smell of the leaves in the shade and on the grass.

22

Later that same day, she wondered where she could find privacy in the house, away from the clamouring children, the questioning women. They had not seen her look like that before: lit up, transformed. They were used to her being a ghost, walking about doing chores, her mind elsewhere, listless, not particularly driven. Now they asked her questions, but she would give nothing away, her dreamy smile, her secret . . . When to find privacy in this house . . . a time of day when she wouldn't be needed, wouldn't be missed. Where to go? Somewhere cool, dim and peaceful.

The television was her friend, the video of the talking baby came to her rescue. Everyone watched enthralled by the charm of Travolta, the beauty of the new mother, the wise words of the infant, translated in Arabic, white words across the bottom of the screen. Mahasen lay on the bed, propped up on one elbow, Hanan was on the opposite bed, a younger mirror image, her husband sat on the armchair with Hassan on his lap and the children were with their egg sandwiches scattered on the floor.

Sammar opened the door of the store room. The musty smell of a room not used, not aired, a smell of dust and rice. She switched the light on. A bulb dangled down from the ceiling, the dust that coated it gave the room a brownish, dull light. Among the large sacks of lentils and beans, among the huge cooking pots that were only needed in special occasions, was the suitcase where her winter clothes were folded up. Her duffle coat, her lined skirts, her gloves, all the clothes she had worn in Aberdeen, the clothes Rae had seen her in. There was dust on the suitcase, with her finger she could write her name through the dust in big loops. But she was here to write in response to Fareed's letter. It was in her pocket now, she had carried it around all day. It was with her when Nahla showed the wedding cards to Mahasen, during lunch, while washing the dishes after lunch, struggling with Amir and his homework . . . It was her secret, she would put her hand in her pocket and feel it, she would take it out and read it at every chance. Every chance. Now it already looked worn out and crumpled: stained with kitchen water, egg from the children's sandwiches, Amir's finger-prints when he had tried to snatch it from her hands while she was helping him with his multiplication homework.

She sat down on the suitcase. Four months ago, that was what Fareed had written, Rae had become a Muslim, he had said the *shahadah* in Fareed's house in Stirling. Why didn't Rae tell her before, why wait four months? To be sure, to make sure that he wouldn't go back on this. He was cautious like that. And now asking . . . It made her smile. She had an airmail letter pad with her, a ball-point pen, two envelopes. She was going to write two letters in two languages. They would say the same thing but not be a translation. She wrote to Fareed first: long and cordial para-graphs, greetings, hoping that his wife and children were well, in good health. When she finished, she folded up the papers, put them in an envelope, wrote out an address in Stirling.

She wrote to Rae. One transparent sheet of airmail paper, a few lines. On the envelope she wrote Aberdeen, Scotland.

Television music came into the room, the voices of *Me And Mama And Travolta*. She unzipped the suitcase and looked at her winter clothes. She unfolded wool and out came the smell of winter and European clouds. She put on her gloves and then took them off, saw her tights, for a year she hadn't worn tights. Her henna-coloured duffle coat, its silky lining. She would wear it again when she went back to Aberdeen, the toggles instead of buttons . . . In one of the pockets, she found the bottle of perfume, oval shaped, amber coloured. She opened it and breathed in, forgot the dust and the smell of dried beans and rice. She ran her fingers over a scarf that was too warm for wearing in Khartoum, its pattern of brown leaves.

Tomorrow, early in the morning she would go to the post office. She would buy stamps. The stamps would be full of colours. A map of the Sudan or jungle animals: an elephant, a rhino, a hippopotamus. She would hold the letters in her hand and in the sunlight stand in front of the post box. Hesitate a little before dropping them in. Then live day after day, get involved in the preparations for Nahla's wedding, and wait. Wait. She had written to Rae, *Please come and see me. Please. Here is where I am* . . .

23

Two weeks later when she dragged open the gate and saw him, they both laughed as if everything was funny. And she was not as shy as she thought she would be, not awkward. He looked older than she remembered and younger too. More white in his hair but looking young because he had travelled a long way and was not diminished or fatigued. He said, 'I've spent all day searching for the house,' and that was funny too. All day searching for the house, her house. All day looking for her and she was not hiding, not masking herself, she was wanting to be found. There were lots of questions for her to ask: what made him lose his way, where was he staying, but they all seemed not to matter, not to be urgent in any way. Just the present, the black metal gate under her hand, warm and streaked by sunlight, dragging it closed again. Their footsteps on the cement of the car-port, their clothes brushing the dust on Hanan's car. They stepped over Amir's bicycle, lying on the steps to the garden. She looked at him and the sun hurt her eyes because she had rushed at the sound of the bell, afraid everyone would wake up and she had forgotten her sunglasses inside.

This was not the usual time for the door bell to ring and bring in visitors. It was after lunch, when the shadow of everything was equal to its height, and she had left everyone asleep, even the children. 'Sleep or else you won't go to Nahla's wedding tonight,' she had threatened them and eventually they had fallen asleep.

She had to leave Rae and go indoors to fetch cushions for the garden chairs, a tablecloth. She had to move carefully so as not to wake anyone up. In the kitchen she hesitated, Pepsi or Miranda? Which would he like more, she should have asked, now she had to guess. Pepsi from the fridge. Ice cubes and she must not make a noise when twisting the ice tray over the sink. Standing in the kitchen with the tap running over the ice, thinking of the next step, a glass, a tray, carrying the ice outside . . . This was abundance after the meagre time, the scratchy, meager time.

In the garden it was easy to talk. Pour the Pepsi into the glass and watch it froth, tiny sprays over the table cloth, then how it effervesced. Talk of the wobbly table, of the cooperative across the road, of Diane's now completed thesis.

Mhairi fell off her horse but she was alright, though she got a scare. He talked about his new students, where they came from, what they were working on. 'I am writing a textbook,' he said, 'an introduction to the politics of North Africa. I've decided it's time for me to write a textbook and not concentrate so much on analysing current affairs.'

He drank his Pepsi and the ice cubes started to melt, their edges smooth and light. 'Is this what you do here,' he said, 'offer guests drinks as soon as they come in and not have anything yourself?'

She smiled and nodded, that was the custom, yes. 'Which airplane did you come on?'

'KLM. I changed planes in Amsterdam. Aberdeen, Amsterdam, then we landed in Cairo on the way, transit for about an hour. I got here at two in the morning.' He smiled and looked at her, 'You were asleep then.'

Two o'clock in the morning she was fast asleep, not hearing the plane that landed in the airport nearby. But later at dawn she had heard the azan and got up to pray. Another dawn, asking for forgiveness, saying there is no will or strength except from Allah, and not knowing, having no idea what the day ahead held out for her.

'Was it alright at the airport?' Sometimes foreigners were given a hard time, their baggage thoroughly and slowly searched, a lot of questions asked.

'Fine, no problems. The conveyer belt wasn't working so it took ages for the luggage to come out but it was okay at the end. It was the smoothest trip I have ever done . . . It must be because my intention is good.'

She smiled and they were quiet for a time. He held the glass in his right hand, as much ice now as Pepsi.

'Why did you tell Fareed to write to me, why didn't you write to me?' She asked without complaint, without reproach. Fareed's letter had been useful: formal, correct, what she needed. She had been able to show it to Waleed and Hanan and say to them, 'You must speak to Mahasen, you must tell her because it would be easier for her if she hears from you.'

'I wanted to do everything properly,' Rae said. 'I was afraid you were married. I would have deserved that . . .'

'No. No, our next door neighbour is getting married.' She still said silly things, unconnected things.

'What's her name?'

'Nahla.' It occurred to her that Nahla was a beautiful name. And it was beautiful that she lived next door and tonight was her wedding. The wide outdoor space of the Syrian club, noisy music and a light wind, everyone wearing cardigans over their best clothes. Rae could go too. She would introduce him to Waleed and everyone she knew.

'And Nahla is your friend?'

'Yes, though she is much younger than me. And she is going to Qatar where Yasmin is.'

'Is Qatar a place you would like to visit?'

'Someday yes.'

Beaming, that was how she was, all over him. She should reproach him for the past, discuss with him practical things. Where was her brain? Yellow grass and the trees untrimmed, a smell she knew, of jasmine and mud.

'I think,' he said, 'we should not prolong this torture.'

'What torture?'

He laughed and wiped his face with his hand. Torture for her were the days when she heard a worldly, logical voice saying, someone like him will never become a Muslim. The voice measured the distance between them, it calculated the probability that he was with someone else, a woman with lighter eyes, a lighter heart . . .

'I mean,' he said, 'if we get married this week, we could go away somewhere. There would be time because I don't have to be back in Aberdeen until the middle of January. I was thinking of Aswan, have you been to Aswan?'

'No.' Her voice was a little subdued because she had remembered the bad voice.

'I haven't been there either,' he said, watching her, the change of expression in her eyes. 'The High Dam is near the town – Nasser's big project. I'm told the south of Egypt is very much like here, in climate and terrain. It would be nice, what do you think?'

She smiled, 'It would be nice.'

'You could leave Amir with your aunt and then we can come back here and all go back together to Aberdeen.'

She nodded but it seemed to her complicated, going north and then coming back to Khartoum. 'It would have been easier that day in Aberdeen, the day of the snow . . .,' her voice trailed. It was the wrong thing to say. He would not want to talk about that day.

When he spoke, his voice was quiet, 'In the Qur'an it says that pure women are for pure men . . . and I wasn't clean enough for you then . . .' He looked up towards the house and Sammar turned to look too. Dalia was walking down the steps of the porch, looking sleepy, her hair sticking out of her braids. She came and sat on the arm of Sammar's chair and put her head on Sammar's shoulder. She stared at Rae, too sleepy to be fully curious.

'Are you still asleep?' Sammar asked her, changing from explaining to Rae who Dalia was, into speaking Arabic. Dalia nodded and rubbed her nose.

'Aren't you going to shake hands?'

Dalia shook her head.

'He knows Arabic,' said Sammar. 'You know Arabic, don't you?' she said to Rae.

'A little, not very much,' he said.

'He can't speak properly,' Dalia whispered in Sammar's ear and made her laugh.

'He needs to practise more,' she whispered back, 'but you should be nice and say salamu alleikum.'

Dalia did, looking more awake, raising her hand a little.

'Alleikum al-salaam,' he replied. She smiled and sat up a little straighter. Her eyes caught sight of Amir's bicycle, lying unwanted and available.

They watched her as she walked away from them, her house-dress crumpled and too small, the zipper at the back a little undone. She rode the bicycle slowly, out of their view, round to the back of the house.

'She will miss you,' Rae said, something final in his voice. Clear to Sammar that she was really going to leave Khartoum and go back with him to Aberdeen. She was going to leave Dalia and not be close to her anymore, the day by day closeness, the eating, sleeping, closeness. She was going to take Amir away from his cousins, his grandmother, his house. She was going to take him to a place that was all grey, its noises muffled by clouds, a new school where they might not like him much, look at him in a surprised way. And she was going to leave this city, its dusty wind and smells.

'If I was someone else, someone strong and independent I would tell you now, I don't want to go back with you, I don't want to leave my family, I love my country too much.' Her voice was teasing and sad.

He did not look taken aback. 'You're not someone else,' he said.

A fly dived silently over the tray and perched on the rim of the empty glass. Sammar leaned and waved it away.

'It's too late now,' he said.

'I know.' She had been given the chance and she had not been able to substitute her country for him, anything for him.

'Ours isn't a religion of suffering,' he said, 'nor is it tied to a particular place.' His words made her feel close to him, pulled in, closer than any time before because it was 'ours' now, not hers alone. And because he understood. Not a religion of pathos, not a religion of redemption through sacrifice.

He said, 'I found out at the end, that it didn't have anything to do with how much I've read or how many facts I've learned about Islam. Knowledge is necessary, that's true. But faith, it comes direct from Allah.'

It was a miracle, she thought. Since getting Fareed's letter she had been waking up in the middle of the night, smiling in the dark, stunned by what had happened, and finding herself unable to go back to sleep.

'When you left,' he said, 'I thought if this isn't enough incentive for me to convert, nothing is, and I felt sick, going around, here and there, no balance.' Once, he said, he missed a flight to Paris. Another conference, another paper to present. He misread the gate number and he was late. He ran, out of breath, along corridors full of people coming back from holidays, cheerful suntans and children holding up big Mickey Mouse balloons. By the time he reached the correct gate, it was too late. He collapsed into a chair and took out his inhaler, to breathe, just to breathe and he watched his plane from the window, reversing and moving away.

'It burned me up. All that running for nothing . . .' he laughed and put his face in his hands. When he looked up at her she was smiling at his description of the frantic corridors full of Mickey Mouse balloons.

Then the time he was ill, he said. Another asthma attack, gales in Aberdeen shaking the trees and him indoors unable to breathe. How long can a night be, how harsh without sleep? Sucking air that would not go in, not go inside. In this helpless state, in this humiliation, the need to pray. This was how it felt, neither lofty nor serene. Not a prayer for the good of humanity nor for successs but just to breathe.

'What I regret most,' he said, 'is that I used to write things like "Islam gives dignity to those who otherwise would not have dignity in their lives", as if I didn't need dignity myself.'

A fly hovered over the tray, buzzing. She waved it away.

He said, 'I was a little taken aback. I didn't think of myself as someone who would turn spiritual . . .'

'I did. I used to feel that there was something inside you very heavy and still.'

'The religious dimension that everyone has?'

'Maybe.' It had seemed to her as something asleep, fast asleep, not moving. Something she had wanted to come close to, stay near, breathing, until it woke.

He said, 'At the end it was one step that I took, of wanting it for myself separate from the work, and then it all rushed to me. It felt like that.'

'What does everyone in the department think about this,' she asked. 'Did you tell them?'

'Yes . . . they think it's mid-life crisis.' He laughed a little and looked away at the cooperative across the road.

She frowned, worrying if in their eyes he had lost his credibility as a detached Middle-east observer. She told him that Yasmin once said, that if he converted it would be professional suicide.

'I've already made a name for myself,' he said. 'Don't worry. I'm not worried.'

He was right, she shouldn't worry, provision came from Allah, it would come from Allah, she shouldn't worry.

She said, 'I admire you so much . . .' and looked down at the grass. When she looked up there was kindness in his eyes and his voice.

Dalia was circling the house with her bicycle, the clatter of wheels on the cement of the car-port. She looked at Sammar and Rae then she disappeared again behind the house.

'There's a rat in my hotel room,' he said. This made her laugh in disbelief and horror and ask, because she had forgotten to ask, which hotel he was staying in?

He named one of the older, more faded hotels overlooking the Nile. Not the best of hotels but still, one that should not have rats running about. He had heard the rat at night, along the wall, near the cupboard.

'That's terrible,' she said, apologetic. This was her country after all, he was her guest.

'The shower doesn't work,' he said. 'That is worse than the rat . . . I think.'

'Did you complain?'

He nodded. 'They promised to fix the shower. They gave me a pail and a pitcher in the meantime. But they didn't seem worried about the rat.'

'I'm sorry,' she said. He had all her sympathy because he looked so resigned.

'The view is great though,' he said. 'The room has a balcony and today at dawn the river . . . it was very picturesque.'

She imagined him standing on the balcony looking out at the Nile. The hotel was built by the British in colonial times. It once glittered and ruled. Now it was a crumbling sleepy place, tolerant of rats and with showers that didn't work. But still the view was as before, something natural brimming over, the last stretch of the Blue Nile before it curved and met with the other river, changed colour and went north.

He talked about the view from the balcony, his first impressions of Khartoum. Last night: the dimly lit airport, the quietness. The taxi driver told him there was a curfew but taxis to and from the airport had passes. On the way to the hotel, they were stopped at a road block, an inspection point. The policeman wore a grey coat, had a gun slung over his shoulder. After an exchange of greeting, he took the pass from the driver, checked it by the headlights of the car. He did not ask Rae for any identification.

'The streets are dark like you said they were,' Rae said. 'It comes as a surprise, this dependence on the moon and stars.'

He would not forget this city, he told her. He would remember it for life. There was something in its air, something bleak and delicate, heightened by the flat desert and the domineering sky. He asked her about Umdurman. Was it far from here?

She said, 'Umdurman is more beautiful. Across the bridge, down the road from your hotel. Saints are buried in Umdurman.'

He said, 'When I was young, my father had old maps. Ones on which Eritrea and Palestine existed. I liked looking at them. I used to see the name Umdurman, written near the blue line of the Nile. I would say Umdurman to myself, over and over again, liking the sound of it.'

They would go and visit Umdurman then, before they left. There were old houses to walk through, a camel market.

She said, 'All the dust here . . . I'm worried that it's bad for your chest.'

'It's not bothering me, my asthma is intrinsic. The dry weather is good for me. It's very dry here I noticed, good for the bones.'

'Old age?' she smiled.

He laughed and said, 'When I started praying my knees hurt, and I also thought "old age", but they don't hurt so much now . . .'

'I missed all that, you learning to pray . . .' The sounds of the garden, a car in the street far away.

'It's a lonely thing,' he said, 'you can't avoid it.'

'What?'

'The spiritual path. Everyone is on his own in this.'

Dalia was trying to haul the bicycle up on to the porch. After some struggle she succeeded and they watched her cycle between the pots of cacti and bougainvillea, wheels smooth on the tiles of the porch.

'*L*et's play a game!' I said. I wanted my eyes to shine and please him. 'We'll give each other thoughts,' he said. 'They would come out of us and then take shape and colour, become tangible gifts.'

'Your turn first,' he said. 'What did you receive from me?'

I showed him three pieces of cloth. I unfolded silk the colour of deserts, mahogany wool, white cotton from a cloud. I said, 'You gave me silk because of how I was created and you gave me wool to keep me warm.'

He said, 'Wool because I want to protect you and cotton because you are clean.'

Then I looked at what he had received from me. The smoothest bowl, inside it a milky liquid, the scent of musk. 'Is it perfume?' I asked, as if I had given birth and now wanted to know if the child I carried for months was a boy or a girl.

'No,' he paused and spoke slowly, 'it is something from you that will make me strong.'

When he named it he looked away as if he was shy. 'Admiration,' he said.